THE ALABASTER GAZE

A NOVEL

SARA YOUSEF

GLOBAL EAST-WEST (GEW) LONDON

ALSO BY SARA YOUSEF

The Unwritten Empire: Abdulrazak Gurnah And The Legacies Of Colonialism. Global East-West (GEW) London,2025. Collection: World Literature.

French translation: L'Empire invisible: Abdulrazak Gurnah et l'héritage du colonialisme (Littératures du monde). Global East-West (GEW),2025.

CONTENTS

PART 1

THE BODY

CHAPTER ONE

THE FIND

(4:30 PM)

When Mary walks into the study, the dim light makes long shadows that look like they are trying to grab her. The air smells harsh and sterile, like a mix of disinfectant and something that is definitely bitter, like metal. Her heart races, but her mind is eerily calm, as if she were watching the scene through a glass wall. Julian is lying there with a mask of peace on his face that makes him look pale and unrecognisable. She has a hard time connecting this person, who used to be full of life and sharp wit, with the shell that is now in front of her. As she gets closer, Mary's hands shake a little. She remembers how warm his laughter was and how his words could tell stories that both fascinated and disarmed her. But now, death has taken over the language of love and life. She bites her lip to keep the wave of sadness that is coming over her from taking over. She knows she has to do something besides give in to the overwhelming feeling of loss that is creeping up her spine. No matter what the truth is right now, something must be done.

Mary holds her breath and pulls her phone out of her pocket. The cool metal feels good against her palm.

She takes a deep breath to slow her heart rate and dials the same three numbers. Each beep makes her think of something else, pulling her further away from the chaos in her chest. The line connects, and all of a sudden, she is thrown into a world of urgency, where sirens and frantic voices make her feel uneasy. The operator keeps asking questions, and Mary answers them quickly and to the point, giving a brief description of what she thinks is a medical emergency. She can hear her voice, but it sounds like someone else's voice, bouncing off the walls of the room, clean and familiar. As she hangs up, a feeling of unreality washes over her, and her heart is still pounding in her ears. She wipes the sweat off her hands on her trousers and stares hard at Julian. She knows that the memory of what she once loved will soon fade under the weight of an investigation, competitors, and her memories that won't go away.

Sloane's breath came in quick, uneven gasps as she stepped lightly over the threshold. The thick, soft rug under her feet muffled each step. The city's usual noise outside faded into a faint murmur, lost in the heavy silence inside the flat. She quickly looked at Julian's laptop, which had a cold, blue light on the screen that made the room feel even more sterile and fake. The air was charged with electricity, like the second before a storm breaks. Everything seemed to be frozen, but Sloane's nerves were anything but. She stared at the messages on the screen for a long time, and the words stuck in her mind with a sharpness she couldn't shake.

At first, the soft click of the keyboard was hesitant, as if she were trying to steady a hand that was shaking and wanted to betray her. Sloane's fingers hovered over the keys as she fought the strong urge to protect herself and the heavy burden of what she was about to erase. That one email, which had thousands of words typed out in anger, fear, or panic, was like a ticking time bomb that was about to destroy everything she had worked so hard to keep together. If she deleted it, she would be closing a door she never meant to open again and cutting the thin thread that connected her financial ruin to a career that was disappearing. She hit the delete key, and the sharp click broke the silence. She watched as the message disappeared into digital nothingness. The emptiness that came after was heavier than the words could ever be. Sloane knew right then and there that what she had done could not be undone.

There was no way to go back and get that piece of truth or change your mind about the decision after it was made. The silence seemed to close in on her, making the faint, distant sound of sirens from the city louder. It was a strange reminder that life was still going on outside of Julian's flat, where everything was polished. But inside, time had stopped, frozen right when she changed everything. When the laptop screen flickered, Sloane realised that some lies, once deleted, could change reality in ways that were impossible to forgive or forget.

Mila pressed on the accelerator, her hands shaking as her consciousness swirled in a maelstrom of fear and regret. The house behind her looked ever more distant in the rearview mirror, yet her thoughts were leaden, choking the roundness of her chest. Each breath she gasped for was shallow, every inhale sharp and rapid as if she couldn't get enough air. Her blood was electrifying now, her limbs heavy and head fluffy. She knew she had to keep a clear head, but the haze of guilt stuck to her like a splinter lodged within her. Now all she could do was run, somehow outrun the horrific mistake that she was sure she had committed.

The car was silent, and suddenly screaming filled her ears from a distance, but as she glanced into the mirror, she could see the first of the ambulances race past her. Its blinker lights sliced through the grey afternoon, throwing fleeting shadows onto the road. Her stomach knotted at the metallic wail of the siren echoing in her ears. She smelt scorched rubber and a trace of gasoline in the air that wafted toward her, as if to remind her that life was suddenly fragile, capricious. The ambulance tearing past made her stomach turn even harder, and it seemed as if her heart was the one pounding in her ears, so loud she couldn't even hear what anyone else might say.

She would rather not turn around, but her eyes flicked toward the mirror, motivated by a jumble of curiosity and dread. The lights bled against the glass, rushing forward and away, a phantom siren that screamed with urgency into the empty room of her mind. Mila gripped the wheel harder as she pressed her foot down more firmly. She tried telling herself to breathe, to settle down, but panic had its grip. Somewhere at the back of her mind, a voice was whispering: What if they find her? What if it all falls apart now? Her mind circled the notion that maybe she was the one truly at fault, though she didn't know exactly how or why. All she knew was that the world outside moved on while she was trapped in a whirlwind of guilt, fleeing from her own shadow.

Her stomach roiled again, and the smell of cold air from the open window mixed with a whiff of exhaust fumes. And as her thoughts ping-ponged between disbelief and terror, Mila began to question whether she'd fled soon enough. Would she run with the evidence, the questions, and the guilty doubts? Or was this merely a fleeting respite—fanning the panic that would drown her? Her fingers wrapped around the steering wheel, knuckles hard with the grip she used to hold back her shaking hands. Her eyes began to swell with her angry tears, but she frantically blinked a lot of them away, concentrating on the road and the faraway wail of sirens that seemed to trail behind her as though it were possessed by an unrelenting spirit. For a moment all she could feel was the crushing weight of her own guilt pushing her down, hurtling at breakneck speed into the void.

The intricacies of human behaviour had always fascinated Detective Denise Byrne. So when an urgent call came in the early hours of a Tuesday morning, her intuition took over. The voice on the other end of the phone was clipped and terse—the sort of crisp tone that betrayed something dark just below its otherwise boring surface. A death under mysterious circumstances in one of the city's wealthiest neighbourhoods. As she wrote down the address, Byrne felt a nagging sense that something was not right about this case. Accidents, suicides, natural causes — she'd been here before, but this seemed different. And the wealth and status of the participants suggested layers behind it all, tension bubbling beneath finances and reputations that could break like glass.

The drive to the scene stretched on, each mile distending her thoughts. She imagined the ladylike, impeccably manicured lawns and sleek facades that defined a neighbourhood in which every window appeared to peek inside and each hedge murmured secrets. As she stepped out of the car, sunlight reflected from sleek surfaces of luxury vehicles lined up like trophies. They appeared beautiful, but Byrne had seen enough to understand that beauty often concealed ugliness. Walking up to the front door was more of a walk onto an elaborate movie set rather than on a crime scene. She opened it, and it creaked, and the sound cut through the quiet like something knew.

Inside the house, marble floors shimmied underfoot, and furnishings were tastefully fussed with as if someone had exacerbated a case of decorative flu by pinning down aesthetic perfection. The walls were hung with beautiful paintings, and every corner of it was daintily adorned in accordance with the life of its occupant, Julian Vane by name, a well-known writer. But Byrne detected something strange behind the there's-a-place-for-everything sheen of this well-groomed façade. It wasn't just the awareness of death poised so close by; there was something else, a formless sadness shrouded in the overly cheerful decor of the living room. A fragile floral arrangement sat on an empty coffee table, its petals too bright and vivid in a desperate attempt to feel alive in a house that felt anything but.

When she went to the interior of the house, her sleuthing intuition turned on. Every room had a story, every detail a possible clue. The subtle aroma of freshly brewed coffee mixed with something more bitter, a hint he couldn't quite put his finger on—that scent stayed just beyond the edge of perception, like a ghost impossible to catch. The corpse was at the end of a long corridor and through the ornate wooden door. But before she entered, Byrne surveyed her surroundings, her brain racing. 'Strange for someone like Julian to be missing family photos on the walls,' she remarked. There was a heavy atmosphere in the air, and it was not just sadness but an unspeakable tension. In the privileged household where prosperity had seemed to flourish, as if with a life of its own, something frightening haunted this woman—and soon Byrne was stripping back layers she might have left in peace.

Chapter Two

THE SCENE

(4:45 PM – 5:30 PM)

Mary was in the bathroom, where the bright white light hurt her eyes and the cold tile floor seeped through her thin slippers. The cold water ran over her hands steadily and without stopping, grounding her in a way that the chaos that had just happened could not. At first, she couldn't believe what had happened. Her chest felt tight, as if it didn't want to accept it. But now, as the shock gradually faded, a clear, practiced calm began to settle over her. It was the same calm she relied on when she scrubbed in before a long procedure, when she had to get rid of all distractions so her hands could move with precision and purpose.

The smell of antiseptic filled the small room. It was sharp and clinical, cutting through the lingering smell of something darker and more personal. Even though she tried to control them, her fingertips shook. The blood that wasn't hers, which was smeared under her nails, kept reminding her. She watched the soapy foam bubble and slip through her fingers. Each scrub was a quiet reminder to herself to stay focused. It was second nature to do it: palms, backs of hands, between fingers, and nails. The touch was mechanical, but inside, a storm of worry grew stronger with each passing second.

Mary's breath caught when the memory of what happened right before came back—Julian's pale face and the way something unreadable twitched in his eyes. She wasn't just washing away a death; she was washing away the weight of everything that had been said and the sudden, unbearable silence that followed. Her hands moved on their own, but her mind raced through options and half-hidden truths. The water was cold, the paper towel was rough as she dried her hands, and there was that impossible stillness, like the moment before a verdict is read, waiting for the storm to break. Those hands, which were steady enough to save lives, now shook with the secret of what had really happened.

Mary let herself feel the edges of panic sharpen for a moment in that sterile space before pulling it back into the tight coil of control she relied on. Cleaning her hands wasn't just about being clean; it was a tentative way to bring order back to chaos. It was a ritual that marked the shift from shock to something harder: resolve. The woman in the bathroom mirror looked calm, but the reflection was a mask that she wore carefully. The weight of the night pressed against her skin, reminding her that no amount of washing could completely wash away what had just happened.

As Sloane reached into the small leather bag she carried with her everywhere, her hands shook a little. She ran her fingers over the cold, rough surface of the envelope she had been hiding for weeks, feeling its weight like a silent burden. There was a piece of paper inside that had been carefully folded and written long before Julian's last day. She wrote it during a quiet time when the house was empty and her mind was racing with fears and doubts. Now, she ran her fingers over the edges of the note, torn between wanting to tell the truth and being afraid of how it might change everything.

There was only one desk lamp in the room, and it flickered, making it dark. Outside, shadows stretched across the walls, thick and heavy, just like the weight in her chest. Sloane's breath caught as she closed her eyes for a moment to calm down. Then she slowly opened the paper. The words she wrote made Julian's last act seem like a tragic but noble sacrifice, a last act of artistic control. It sounded like he was confessing to his own despair, a desperate plea wrapped in poetic language that only someone who knew him well could understand. She stiffened when her fingers touched the ink, remembering how Julian had thought about each word: what he wanted to say, what he hoped to say, and the harsh truth that lay beneath the lines.

She took a deep breath and carefully put the note in a plastic sleeve to keep it safe. There was a mix of hope and fear in her eyes as she looked at it. She walked slowly to Byrne's office, taking her time and being careful. The house was so quiet that the only sounds were the old radiator's low hum and the pounding of her own heart. Sloane could feel the weight of what she was about to do as she finally walked into the room where Byrne was going over files. She broke the silence with a soft but steady voice as she slid the note across the desk with a shaking hand. She watched Byrne's face closely, looking for any sign of recognition or suspicion. Her nerves were on edge with hope that this piece of paper might finally change the story of Julian's death from an accident or illness to the truth: his carefully planned suicide, which he had to answer for.

The investigator read the carefully chosen phrases on the page, and her eyes narrowed as she did. The air was thick with unspoken secrets, and the room turned uncomfortable. Sloane's voice shook a little bit as she told Julian why she thought he was a tragic hero instead of someone who died in an accident. She added that Julian's last act showed his artistic integrity, even if it was too painful for him to do. Each line was intended to convince Byrne that Julian's death was not an accident but the product of a long-planned decision, with equal parts conviction and vulnerability. Byrne read the note carefully, and the words hung in the air, heavy and not clear. Her eyes flickered with doubt and a glimmer of understanding that made Sloane clutch her breath, wondering if her truth was finally breaking through the wall of doubt.

Mila sat on her old couch, and the TV's faint light formed shadows that moved about on the walls. Every second that made her heart race made her worry more and more. The news anchor's voice was silky, yet it sounded like the words were trapped in her throat. Julian Vane, the person who had once inspired her to write, was dead. The details were coming out like a train crash in slow motion, and she couldn't look away. People were talking about whether it was suicide, an accident, or something much worse. Her mind got more and more muddled as she heard fragments of their last chat in her head. Things had changed since then, and now they felt like a distant echo, full of melancholy and doubt.

The reports had a lot of information about his death, which was still a mystery. The flat was unnaturally quiet except for the news segment that was still playing on, which just made her head feel more confused. She didn't even notice the cup of old coffee that was cold and forgotten on the table. In addition to the sour taste of anxiety still in her throat, there was the smell of bitterness. Was this the conclusion of Julian's final big work? Or were they just parts of his big story? Mila's stomach turned. She could feel anxiety crawling up her back, combining with the pain of losing someone. It was too much to deal with. She felt horrible about how it would affect her if he died. What would happen if everyone knew she was seeing him? She felt entirely alone in the silence after the report.

Detective Byrne walked into the living room, and her

boots barely made a sound on the polished wood floor. The air inside was strangely calm, with no sign of the chaos she had expected to find. There was no mess or signs of struggle; instead, every surface shone. The air was sterile and quiet, as if someone had scrubbed away not only dirt but also any sign of life or conflict. The couch was perfectly arranged, with the cushions just the right amount of fluff, and not a single book or piece of paper was out of place. There was even a faint smell of lemon-scented cleaner in the air. It was sharp and clean, cutting through the dull heaviness that usually filled rooms where something bad had happened. The impression was disturbing—too neat, too exact—like a stage set frozen in time, waiting for actors who had already left.

Byrne's eyes moved slowly, taking in things that shouldn't be there or might be missing. She noticed a half-full glass on the side table, but it looked like no one had touched it. The light made the liquid shine. The curtains were pulled back, letting in a lot of light, but the light didn't do anything to warm up the walls. It was as if everything had been wiped clean of panic or haste, which was something Byrne was used to feeling when he was near death. She knew what a crime scene looked like right after it happened: a mess of things, with quick movements showing up as disorder. Nothing moved here. The silence was heavy, like the lack of a heartbeat on her chest.

She took a slow breath. There was a faint metallic smell in the air that made her nose tingle, but it was so faint that she thought it was just her imagination. The house, which was supposed to be a safe place, felt wrong. Byrne had been in a lot of homes before, where people were angry, scared, sad, or desperate. But this one was too clean and too calm. That perfect calm felt like a mask stretched tight over something much more complicated underneath.

Mary West sat perfectly still in an armchair across the room. Her posture was straight and unyielding, and she was as calm as a surgeon before a delicate operation. Her fingers tapped a rhythm on the armrest, but her face showed no signs of chaos. There was no sign of shock in her voice when Byrne came in quietly. Mary's calmness hit a nerve. It was a practiced calm that didn't come from accepting things but from carefully holding them. Her lips were pressed together in a thin line, and her eyes were fixed ahead with the steady gaze of someone who had practised this moment over and over, hiding what was going on inside. The difference between the calm around her and the storm Byrne felt inside was sharp, like glass about to break.

Byrne's instincts were uneasy around Mary. She had seen grief before, in its raw, rough, and sometimes violent forms, but this was different. Mary's calm hid more than her sadness; it was a wall of distance. Mary held herself in a clinical way, as if she were watching a situation that she needed to control at all costs. She was calm but alert. It wasn't the calm that comes after a traumatic event when you're confused. This was a planned stillness that made Byrne's skin crawl. Mary's silence spoke louder than any words. Something was wrong.

Byrne squinted as she looked at the woman she knew was the deceased's closest friend. Every little thing about this fragile moment felt wrong, like how Mary's breath didn't hitch and she didn't cry even though she was so sad. It was like Mary was behind a glass wall, untouchable and separate, keeping herself safe from any truth that might come out. Byrne could tell that someone was very upset but was determined to keep up an unbreakable front.

THE "TRUTH" OF THE DEATH

Mary kept still in the interview room, her fingers trembling as she prepared. Her voice was steady, but it also seemed brittle, every word considered as she relayed what had happened that morning. Julian, she said, had grown increasingly fatigued in recent weeks as he experienced what doctors called a neurological decline. As stubbornly as he interjected that she did not want to take the advice, she had encouraged him to do so and watched him refuse it with a strong, almost defiant shove. This morning he had turned everything away — the pills, his breakfast, her attempts to keep him company. She recalled feeling a twinge of frustration but thought he just wanted to be alone. When she went to check on him an hour later, he was still in their bedroom, looking the same as when she left him but no longer breathing, and it gave her an enduring feeling that the end had come quietly, naturally — no drama or warning — from a cause larger than themselves.

Her words sketched a man wearied, delicate, maybe reconciled. She stressed that, although he had declined to medicate himself, he had shown no sign of immediate distress. She was simply attuned to how calm he seemed and how evenly he was drawing breath, and she had no reason to expect anything was wrong until she thought him unresponsive. But beneath her measured tone, there was a glimmer of something else — an undercurrent of anxiety she couldn't quite disguise. Her notes shook in her hands, and her voice stuttered as she recounted calling emergency services, what they did to extend life – and how she tried to help – and a sense of creeping sensation that this was just another day in their slow, steady march toward the inevitable end. Her story was supposed to be simple — a run-of-the-mill, natural death, nothing shady or strange about it, just an old man who decided to go to sleep and slip away.

"You came here because you've heard my offer and that I was not one to hide in the flanks, yes, probably drink in hand," Mary said. It sent her voice off balance for a second, and she hated it. What she said seemed canned and too good to be true – but her hands would give her away. They shook just enough to catch the eyes of investigators, who were closely watching her. Her manner was professional, her head down, describing

Julian's descent as if she were reading a medical report and studiously avoiding any acknowledgement of emotional ties or personal feeling. All the details of medication schedules, his weak grip and slow, overt movements were treated as factual. She wanted the authorities to witness a man at the end of his life, descending peacefully into age and illness. But beneath that shroud of disengagement, a tremor of unease still lingered — was it sorrow or shame? Her mind buzzed with thoughts of what there would be to find out about that morning, about whether her own secret worry—that Julian might need some medicine he wouldn't take—would be brought to light.

However, her attempt to look composed was a transparent ploy meant to divert attention away from the kind of natural death that would cause officers to set sights on her. Her words were precise, and she was reigning herself in from even a whiff of premeditation or foul play. But her heart took off in a drumroll every time she thought about the small bottle of pills in her medical kit when she remembered pushing the same vial Julian had pushed away that morning. She was afraid that her own nervousness would be confused for guilt — or that her measured, calm story wouldn't sate the officers' curiosity and the case would drag on. She was aware that they would be able to find her internal torment in them if they searched hard enough, but she hoped for the time being this pathetic offering would keep up the pretence of it all being one of life's letting go.

In feeling the tension of that moment, she held on to the hope that her story would be sufficiently in line with Stewart's version to keep her reputation intact and that, rather than looking foolish, her professional distance might appear justified. But she also had to learn how to navigate through the disturbing uncertainty of the fact that her own suppressed fears — of failure and of losing control over Julian's health — could unravel everything if exposed. So she kept her cool, a professional shell hiding the approaching storm inside, speaking in calm, measured tones and still as her stomach began to twist with a creeping sense of decay.

Sloane stood in Julian's dark study, the air thick with musty books and ink that had dripped from a toppled jar. She remembered the worried frown that would wrinkle his forehead as he tapped his fingers anxiously on his desk while tensing under the weight of people's expectations. He fed off the tension but also suffocated from it. In her mind, Julian was a man trapped in an endless blizzard of creation and despair, fighting invisible forces as the reigning literary superstar. The world was demanding great things from him, and the weight of that burden clung to his soul like a chain.

The note he left wasn't just words written on paper; it was a window into his troubled head and heart. It was everything Sloane had been fighting to understand. Each line sounded like an entreaty, a confession that cut to the core of his own torments. She read the symptoms of a man overburdened, at risk from his own making. For a moment she knew that Julian's choice to do away with himself was one of desperation, not cowardice, an effort to seize the narrative back from a story he'd lost control of.

His final note, the last note he wrote, was his touching goodbye to Julian, a heartfelt expression of his internal struggle with a world that wouldn't let him be. Sloane could remember his voice wobbling with vulnerability in their conversations. His words, however painful, had a haunted beauty that exposed a mind brilliant and tortured. She could not rid herself of the sense that he considered his death a dramatic gesture, the last theatrical act of defiance to what suffocated him, evidence of his anguish and art in one gesture.

Sloane was pissed off and sad all in one sitting. It was just not right to lose your father like this. She knew how prone those left would be to misread his actions — how many people would rather this be a tragedy than a complex, conscious choice. Julian's death was not just a point of despair; it was an unspoken statement about the price of genius, and it forced us to recognise the desperate lengths he went to in order to get out from under a situation that had become unbearable. Julian meant this; Sloane understood. This was a statement he wanted remembered long after he was gone.

The day comes back to Mila in bursting, jagged pieces of memory. The sound of Julian's voice cracking hard and brittle, like shattered glass snapping at her across the dark room. Angry words crackled between them, Tamashek'a, words like blows that landed harder and quicker until every nerve was taut and the tension exploded into action. The fight hadn't been planned or even particularly conscious at first—it was raw, a violent and sudden geyser of anger and frustration breaking through the rotten shale of too much that had come between them. Then her hand came up, almost instinctively, the shove rapid and thoughtless. Julian staggered back, eyes wide with shock, off-centre enough that the corner of the desk was suddenly right there in his face, looming as a silent, dooming threat. Everything seemed to be in slow motion—the hard smack of his elbow against the wood, a dull thud as his head hit the floor.

She recalls the cold sweep of desperate panic that passed through her — her heart thumping so loudly it was as if everything else had been drowned out. A silly, stupid action: A push that she regretted immediately; she hadn't meant for it to go this far. She froze, the room tightening around her, air thick and sour with guilt and shock. Julian didn't lose it to having wanted harm; she lost a moment in fear and confusion because something darker had remained, something she hadn't wanted to confront. It happened so fast that part of her wondered if she had dreamed the whole thing, something she could blink away. But the blood soaking the floor told her it wasn't and kept her rooted in dark reality. The moment was another degree beyond argument or blame. It was an accident. Her accident.

Even in the midst of everything that was happening, Mila found her mind racing to put together what had transpired on that tangled afternoon. The fight hadn't been plucked from the ether—years of frustration, muttered recriminations and unspoken betrayals led to that small but intense confrontation. And there was something raw in Julian's eyes, normally so calculating and unreadable — a touch of betrayal, a hint of demand, in those last moments. She still heard his gasp of breath when she had pushed back, trying to shove him away, and he, the jerk, fell for it. There was no advance planning, just a stupid, fear-fuelled rush of blood that quickly spun out of control. That shove changed everything. It broke the tenuous equilibrium that they had kept, forcing themselves to maintain, setting off a shockwave neither was capable of handling.

The guilt is a leaden weight Mila carries, a constant companion she cannot shake. Again and again she reminds herself it was an accident, that she never meant to hurt Julian, but every time the moment replays in her head, that sharp edge of self-reproach pierces deeper. Fear drove her—fear of losing everything she'd earned, fear of Julian's darkness swallowing everything else up. She was frightened then, and her legs burnt with the desire to run, cold sweat slick on her skin. And then she ran — not just from the room, but from her own conscience, knowing that she was now enmeshed in a lie built on confusion and error. The crash wasn't just the literal fall; it was how immediately her life broke apart afterward, how every primal, animalistic instinct in her told her to run away before the truth could catch up.

The truth of that isn't easy for Mila's mind to square, because fear and memory are sly allies. She wasn't being cold and calculating; she was unmediated, a mess of raw emotions, flailing around to fend off the early disintegration of the world. She feels the awesome weight of responsibility that has crushed her and what fear did to distort her perception and dull reason. It was never to be this way—with Julian on the ground and her right in the middle of something so much larger than either one of them. She knows the fight, the push, and the accident—they are pieces of a puzzle that no longer fit together neatly, shards of memory fragmented by panic and pain. It's all so hazy. Clarity feels like a million miles away, trapped under guilt and denial that she battles each day to remove the layers off of.

As Mila reflects on the event for herself, she also faces the ways memory can warp and betray. Time does what it always does in such life-or-death situations: It blurs the edges of what really happened, twisting moments into shapes that suit survival rather than truth. She can't help but second-guess the specifics—how hard Julian shoved her, what his words really sounded like, and even the order in which things unfolded. It's an awkward dance between what really happened and what her mind permits her to recall. This doubt nibbles at her, nourishing the fear that perhaps it was no accident after all or, worse, that it was something much more deliberate than she can acknowledge. The boundaries of fear, shame and reality become blurred, forming a tale that imprisons then frees her from her deepest secret.

To live with that kind of accident is to dwell in the relentless realisation that one moment, one tiny mistake, and lives will never be the same. She can never go back; she cannot undo what happened the second that Julian pushed her. Instead there is only, in the aftermath, an echo—a hollow emptiness afterward, a sour taste of remorse and then ceaseless replaying of what happened in the mind's eye. Mila's story is a potent reminder that accidents leave scars that go well beyond the visible kind. They cut into a person's soul, the way they live, love and remember. The truth persists in the tangle of human emotions, unable to escape the grip of fear, confusion, and the unavoidable need to survive.

Detective Byrne, who scrutinises the stories put before her with a gimlet eye, observes something disquieting about how everyone describes things as they were. Each person's narrative sounds rehearsed, polished, and oddly identical, as if they have rehearsed their lines for at least 20 hours. There is a kind of inflexibility in the narrative, like masks obscuring their true emotions. It's uncanny how perfectly smooth their stories are: there are no stumbles, no pauses, no glints of real feeling. Byrne can feel that beneath the glossy veneer, these narratives are manufactured, each one shaped to slot seamlessly into a crafted image.

Comparing them to these polished accounts, she feels they are only the surface of something darker. The deeper she digs, the clearer it is that each of these stories is missing something crucial. The specifics don't even match up exactly for her, and the inconsistencies start to bubble up if she examines them all closely. She has seen other instances where people lie — sometimes poorly, sometimes dangerously — but these stories just seem too pat, too rehearsed. Instead, it's as though all parties involved have strived to produce a version that seems seamless. Byrne's intuition suggests that beneath those well-rehearsed stories, the actual truth is waiting patiently behind a smokescreen. No one is telling the full story, perhaps because reality has been too grotesque or simply too delicate to speak out loud.

My guess is that the true lie is deeper than words on a page. It's not only about who might be lying, but why they are lying and what they're trying to shield. She observes that the attempts to create an innocent front are observed even in petty things, but we never noticed it, but they tell us so much more beyond. Mary appears to be the calm one, but she is obscuring her fear for Julian's health; Mila frantically denies what she already knows will come out and the guilt she isn't prepared to admit. Every story is about covering something up, something disturbing: a motive, a past event or an action committed in a split-second frenzy. Byrne knows that for someone to present such clean, unadulterated stories, there has got to be a messy and complicated truth hiding behind them. Her role is to strip away those layers and reveal what lies beneath the veneer of perfection.

In her experience, when stories are this neat, there's usually something unspeakably rotten underneath. Sometimes, a detail remains unnoticed until you bring it up, as it contradicts the narrative they are trying to promote. Then there are other times when it's a note of nervousness in their voice, or perhaps the momentary pause they take before responding, that makes clear while they might project confidence on the outside, such confidence inside is anything but sturdy. Byrne has learnt to listen to those small clues, those microexpressions, the inconsistencies in language, or the way certain things are over-explained. This instinct has proven invaluable to her numerous times, particularly when confronted with individuals intent on convincing her of their innocence. When the narrative coming from someone is unhealthily perfect, Byrne knows it's time to call into question everything and also read between the lines about what they are actually hiding.

But even with her experience and intuition, she made it easy to be overwhelmed by how plausible these stories sounded. They sound so carefully rehearsed. It's simple to get swept up in their stories, especially when the person telling them has a stable countenance and an unshaken voice. But Byrne's training has taught her that consistency is no evidence of honesty — it frequently indicates the opposite. When the narratives are this neat and deceptively tidy, it's almost always a sign of what they're hiding. A genuinely honest person typically stumbles over details or feels uncomfortable. But these witnesses seem too good to be true, so Byrne is left with the unsettling idea that these tales are just a cover for something deeper, and the truth is hidden in the gaps between their words.

The burden ends up being to sift through what is real

and what isn't. To remind herself of this, Byrne must remember that people lie not so much because they are evil, but rather because they seek protection or want to avoid shame. Here, she asks whether the tales are meant to cover up a disastrous miscalculation, an act of despair or a thoughtfully choreographed spectacle. Each word, and movement seems planned. It is as though they are all playing a game, each of them trying to outsmart her by pretending to be honest. But the reality is unclear, hidden by lies that everyone has built to protect their interpretations of events.

Ultimately, Byrne's job is to look beneath the surface, identify the false perfection, and discover the cracks through which bits and pieces of actual life can leak. Only then can she know what was really going on during those last minutes of Julian Vane's existence—if, indeed, the truth of that has any real existence outside the vain imaginativeness everyone is grasping at so despairingly!

Chapter Four

THE FIRST CONTRADICTION

Detective Byrne bore down on her, locking eyes with Mary. The room felt electric in its silence, mingling their breaths together into the still air. Mary looked in the orderly manner of a woman wearing a fresh white blouse — looking not at all like the maelstrom within. Under her composed surface, there were traces of concern on her face. Byrne was not only set to peel away those layers, she was going to lay bare what was beneath. The "natural causes" theory of Julian's death had been comforting for Mary, an avenue for avoiding the complexity of Julian's end. But Byrne wasn't buying it. Circumstantial evidence created a barrier between them that prevented Mary from maintaining her facade.

"You're sure he didn't have any suicidal tendencies?"

The question was a heavy one, and it weighed in the air. Mary hesitated, her throat tightening.

"Julian was a very brilliant man, but he was struggling," she finally said, her voice quivering a bit.

The detective noticed the flash of raw emotion behind the mask Mary had erected in her eyes. Byrne pushed back, pointing to a set of anomalies, such as the absence of Julian's bottle of pills and his recent manuscript that contained hints of despondency. Every piece of evidence was like a grain of sand in the walls that Mary built around her story, ready to come tumbling down at any moment.

Mary's heart had beaten faster with every fresh detail. Byrne laid out the tragic facts like a deck of cards, each representing another possible indictment.

"What about the bruising on his body, Mary?"

She was shocked by the forwardness of the question. Her breaths came in a steady rhythm, but now they dipped slightly. She tried to speak, but no coherent words came out. Rather, it was images of Julian, defenceless and sick, that crowded her thoughts. She retreated to her explanation of natural causes and grasped it like a lifeboat in storm-tossed waters. Yet even as she spoke, she felt the gravity of her own words, knowing the fissures that undermined her narrative.

The tension in the air crackled as they exchanged words. Byrne leaned further across the table, her voice becoming a whisper, almost conspiratorial.

"You can't run from the truth all your life, Mary. You are not just saving yourself; you're standing between Julian's story and how the world will understand this case."

Those words were like a sudden gust of cold wind blowing over Mary: it upset the balance she believed she had so nicely kept. She felt the walls closing in on her, the accusations sifting through the air like a mesh. This was not simply a war of words. It seemed more like the minute when truth squared up against the tortured narrative she had constructed to protect herself from Julian's death.

Sloane sat stiffly in Byrne's messy office, where the smell of old paper and stale coffee filled the air. Byrne walked slowly in front of her desk, making every step count, like a predator closing in. Her eyes didn't quite meet the detective's. The walls were covered in pinboards full of photos, notes, and timelines, and they felt like they were closing in on her with each pointed question that Byrne threw at her. Even though she wore a calm mask—a tight-lipped smile and a cool gaze—the tension underneath flickered like a candle trying to stay lit in the wind. Byrne could hear the doubts behind her carefully crafted defence, even though her silence was almost louder than her words.

Byrne said softly, with her arms crossed: "You say Julian fell, but the way you tell it—quickly, neatly, and without a hitch—doesn't add up."

Sloane, this isn't just about grief. Something's not right. For a moment, the agent's confidence wavered, and her fingers nervously brushed the edge of the armrest. She pressed her lips together tightly, as if she were trying to keep a secret, but Byrne heard it in her voice when she answered. The detective leaned in and narrowed her eyes. *Tell me the truth. Was it suicide or something else? Did he fall, or did someone push him?*

The air between them got thicker with suspicion and

unspoken accusations. Sloane's mind raced to find ways to fix holes in her story. But Byrne wasn't just questioning what she said; she was also questioning the parts she didn't say. The more Byrne pushed, the more the thought of suicide started to fade, and a darker doubt took its place. Was Julian's death a carefully planned event? A sad accident that looks like the end? Byrne's gut told her that the neat story Sloane told was precisely what Julian wanted everyone to believe: a story made to protect or maybe even control.

Sloane worked hard to stay calm. She wrapped herself in rehearsed explanations and long pauses that barely hid how upset she was. Her voice was steady but fragile, like glass that had been carefully handled. But when the agent told Byrne about Julian's last day, he saw a hint of a contradiction. The moments didn't fit together as well anymore. Some fell, and some crashed into each other. She discussed a conversation with Julian that Byrne knew was impossible, or at least very out of order based on the statements that were collected. The detective's eyes narrowed as she felt the line between reality and fantasy getting bigger.

Byrne said softly: "These inconsistencies aren't mistakes. They are important. How did Julian fall if he didn't jump? And why would you keep the details a secret?"

The questions were difficult to answer. The quiet room filled with tension, like the calm before a storm. Byrne was looking closely at the idea of suicide, which was so simple and neat. Instead, death seemed to be shrouded in lies and shadows. It looked like Julian set up the fall and left pieces behind for other people to pick up, misunderstand, and fight over. A plan not only to kill him but also to entirely change the story of his death.

Byrne's discoveries complicated the story. For example, there was the missing footage from the security cameras, the messages Julian deleted from his phone, and the fact that there were no final goodbye notes. Sloane's appeals to keep things calm and polite now felt like a ploy to safeguard a weak, made-up story. The garden outside the window, where Julian purportedly breathed his last breath, didn't feel like a site of mourning anymore. It felt like a stage where truth was bending and slipping away. Byrne realised that this case wasn't only about death; it was also about who gets to write the finale when the author is gone and who is in charge.

Mila sat at her little kitchen table, and the sound of the city outside the open window was very faint. The morning light spilt over the wood, making soft shadows that moved with the wind. But even though the scene was calm, her mind was racing. Her fingers lightly tapped on her mug while she stared at the glowing screen of her phone. It felt like there was a static charge in the air that made her skin tingle and her stomach tighten. She had learnt a long time ago that mornings like this had a certain weight to them, a silent sign that something was wrong. Today, her nerves were so tight that she could almost hear them snap.

She was in a trance when her phone buzzed out of the blue. She thought about it for a moment before grabbing it, her heart racing. She saw a flashing message on the screen that said it was an urgent news alert. She quickly unlocked her phone and saw the headline in big, scary letters:

"Foul Play Suspected in Julian Vane's Death." The words made her body feel like it was going to explode. She had a hard time understanding what she was reading. People thought Julian's death would be a quiet, natural event that could be easily explained. But now, someone was saying that something awful had happened, something that made her stomach turn cold.

For a moment, the words on the screen were difficult to read because her hands were shaking. Her heart raced faster and faster with each passing second, and her breath hitched. She looked at the screen, and all she could think about was, "Could this be real?" Was Julian's death not an accident after all? Panic took hold, gripping her with cold hands. Her mind was racing, going from one idea to the next. Who could be to blame if something bad happened? Was someone trying to hide the truth because it would hurt too much? She felt a sudden wave of fear, like the wind rushing through a broken window, cold and never-ending. This was no longer news; it was a threat.

She held the phone tightly in her hands, and her knuckles turned white as she tried to calm her shaking voice. She knew she had to move quickly. It wasn't clear if the leak was real yet, but that didn't matter. Her mind was full of pictures—Julian dead, his last moments full of secrets. She thought back to the last time she saw him. He looked worn out but still sharp, and his thick glasses hid his eyes. In her mind, those eyes looked empty, as if he had known everything that was going to happen. She thought that someone in Julian's group might know more than they were letting on and have a reason to keep the story hidden or twist it into something malicious. Fear crept into her mind: had she missed all the signs?

Mila's heart raced in her ears as she sat there, realising that her world had just changed. This leak of information could reveal things that should remain hidden, things that could change everything she thought she knew about Julian. She was so nervous about what to do next that her stomach hurt. Could she keep quiet? Or would she be guilty of a terrible lie if she stayed quiet? The questions came at her so quickly that she couldn't catch them. She only knew that her sense of safety was falling apart around her, along with the life she had carefully built and the secrets she had kept. The silence in her house now felt deafening, with only the steady, unending pounding of her panic. She knew that once a piece of truth gets out, it can never be fully contained again. Her gut told her that this was just the start of something much worse.

Detective Byrne got out of her car, and the cool air of the early evening wrapped around her like a blanket.

As she walked towards the sprawling estate, the air was thick with tension. The cold air was sharp, and the smell of blood made her shiver. The faint smell of Julian Vane's expensive cologne still hung in the air as she stepped inside the house. It clashed with the sterile smell of hospital disinfectant that filled the rooms. Her instincts kicked in, and she could feel the tension in her muscles as she looked around at the scene, which was a mix of luxury and despair.

The living room, which used to be a place where people could be creative and work together, was now a silent witness to horror. The furniture was arranged neatly, but it felt like it was out of place in the middle of the chaos that was about to happen. As the forensic team diligently worked around her, Byrne's gaze remained fixed in the centre of the room. Julian lay on the floor, dead, with a final act going on around him. She thought about how different his life had been from the end of it all, which made her more determined to figure out what had just happened.

The medical examiner, a methodical man with years of experience written around his eyes, started to explain the troubling news. His voice was low but firm as he said, "Blunt force trauma to the head." The words hung in the air like a dense fog, yet what was true was more essential. He discussed the forceful break in Julian's skull, which indicated that he had been fighting and being aggressive.

Then he went on to make a grim confession: he had taken too many prescription drugs. The effects were huge. Evidence pointed to this not being a case of careless self-sabotage but rather a planned move, which suggested that the administration was involved. As the details came out, whispers of what Byrne wanted to do slipped through his mind like tendrils of smoke. Every piece of information was part of a larger story that needed to be told. She looked around the room again, her senses heightened as she tried to remember the moments before this tragedy. She was looking for every silent clue that would help her put together the last act of Julian's life.

This scene was full of raw emotion and hidden motives, and as every theory raced through her mind, Byrne knew she was on the edge of something very disturbing. Each character had a story that twisted through love, ambition, and betrayal. The keys to untangling the web of humanity were locked in this quiet room, and she was determined to find them.

CHAPTER FIVE

THE GLASS

There was a grating of keys in the lock, and as Mary sprang to her feet, the door creaked open: shadows long and blackened stretched into the untidy room. It smelt of old paper mixed with something metal, and the scent made her want to go deeper, below all these rooms that were acting so prim and well-behaved even if the back of her neck felt tingly. The dim light was slow to register on her eyes. And when they did, they found Julian lying on the floor: limp, colourless and eerily silent. She looked down and saw broken glass all over his body, and her chest grew heavier. And the small fragments glittered in the dark: parts of something that could not be repaired, which made her feel worse.

The glass was meant to be for one, and it should have been perfect—ordinary, even—a plain crystal glass from Julian's favourite whisky set. Now it was shattered and at his side. The rupture felt sudden and violent, a stark contrast to the body's calm stillness. They had such odd angles that when the dim light caught the broken bits of crystal, pale rainbows touched down on the worn floorboards. Mary's fingers itched to wrap around them, but her mind was exploding in a whirlwind of shock and disbelief as she attempted to interpret exactly what had just occurred.

She gasped when she noticed a dark spot spreading across one of the shards of glass. At first, it was nothing more than a faint glimmer. Then the redness was visible, fingerprints smeared all over. Her heart began to pound, and each thrum felt like a drum in her ears. She automatically leant over and brushed the glass with trembling fingers, careful not to disturb it any more than was necessary. It was almost cruel, the chill of the glass on her skin. The blot dissipated, and the picture brightened and grew solid.

She was attempting to maintain some calm, for at that time sheer panic had been climbing up inside her like an animal in a cage. Her brain exploded and flung itself into pieces—what had she done? Did Julian get hurt? Was he still alive? The cold, sterile half of her mind that functioned on pure medicine was screaming for her to do something, but the part of her that knew him—her husband she thought she had so completely and totally known it all—was screaming betrayal and confusion. Her breathing was now ragged, the walls of the room closing in. The old clocks' ticking became a steady countdown.

Mary's eyes darted about the room, searching for something solid in the chaos. The shattered glass on the ground, Julian's lifeless body, and his outstretched arm as if trying to reach for something just beyond her grasp all combined to create a horrifying tableau she wasn't sure she could process. Her fingers trembled, and the cold sweat on her skin felt like it would make her explode. Her brain was desperately trying to figure out how she could render the calm, composed person she presented to the world as something that made sense with what was about to happen next, which was that she would be raw and vulnerable with shock. For a moment, she wanted nothing more than to look away and pretend it wasn't there, but something held her fast – a silent determination to hear the entire story, no matter how grim.

Despite her fear, Mary did what she could to understand what had happened with the same minute detail a doctor would go on to use. Was the blood new? Was it like Julian's injury? She glanced over her shoulder at the glass and where the light played against the ghost images of dust or fingerprints, evidence of a struggle no one witnessed or a desperate move. Little things – people hadn't noticed them, but they were the ones that told secrets in a room that was hushed. As she steadied her trembling hand to clean the last smudge from the glass for a second time, every possibility raced through her mind: an accident of clumsiness, a deliberate act of despair, or something more sinister concealed beneath layers of polished deceit.

Now it was fear mingling with confusion and something sharper — a pain that settled low in her chest. It was impossible to predict what would happen next, besides the shattered glass and the motionless man beneath it. The panic never left; it worsened and carried her aloft, naked: no filters. But, however insane things were, a small voice inside her said, 'Shut up and watch and take command.' She gave the glass a quick polish and wiped it dry to ensure that there was no residue of her being there. This was an odd combination of a desire to protect and expose the truth.

There was a terse, stifling silence before the noise returned in full force: the ticking clock, her own rapid breathing, and the faint drone of the house creaking. But Mary could feel that the panic was not only a reaction but also the beginning of something's falling apart. How she managed this moment, with the shattered shards in her hand, would cast a long shadow over everything that followed. At times like these, even the smallest fragment of evidence — a fingerprint smeared on shattered glass — can unlock a story nobody wants to tell.

Sloane noticed that Mary had picked up the glass again. Her hand was steady, but her eyes betrayed an occasional hint of doubt. She was doing it so slowly and with such care that it seemed deliberate the way she wiped the condensation off. No rush, no fast dab to clear her view. Instead, there was one sluggish, almost ritual swing that Sloane took notice of. It was as if Mary was attempting to cover over whatever her true sentiments were; she was trying to smooth something out that was going on inside. Sloane understood this was more than cleaning; it was a shield, an act that kept her mind in check while she protected herself from the vulnerability she feared most.

For each stroke of the cloth, Mary appeared to be in control of her respiration as she moved with an almost mechanical precision. For a brief moment she looked to the window, then back at the glass, as if working out what came next or how much to say. Sloane had watched more than enough people keep secrets to recognise this delicate dance — these small, choreographed acts that speak volumes. It wasn't just that she wanted clear glass; it was about the illusion of calm, which she very much wanted. Perhaps Mary was trying to protect herself, Sloane thought, or else Julian himself — whose last moments looked as if they had been scratched on a door in the corridor.

Wiping became more than a cleaning action and instead turned into a silent, tense ritual fraught with subtext. Mary pushed with a sense of purpose and control, as if she were acting with each sweeping motion not just to erase smudges. It dispelled doubts, guilt and fears. She may have been protecting her secrets, or she may have had something that could ruin everything. Sloane's eyes remained on Mary for a long time, and she saw the slight tremble of her fingers at the end of each stroke, which proved that despite her confident look, she wasn't feeling as calm as she looked. That made Sloane consider the shadows behind her smooth face and what secrets she fought ever so diligently to conceal.

It was evident that Mary was doing more than just wiping. It was her way to protect herself and walk away from that experience. Everything she did seemed done to ward off anything unsettling, to conceal a slip, a crevice in her armour. And Sloane also knew that what people didn't say was often louder than what they did in cases like this. That cloth was not just a tool; the way she handled it gave her control. Sloane wondered what Mary was really thinking. Was she keeping Julian's secrets safe, her own secrets safe, or perhaps a bit of both? Whatever it was, Sloane knew that this simple act of wiping the glass meant more than any words ever could.

Each time the cloth was passed around, the tension in the room increased. Sloane was convinced that what Mary did in her ritual was, in a primordial way, an act of self-defence. Wiping that had kept her guilt, shame, and growing fears at bay... Fears that were slowly eroding the calm mask she was wearing. She seemed to be trying to wipe from her eyes not just dust or mist but also the traces of her own unassuaged nervousness. It was one of those moments that Sloane intuited was the real key to knowing her and seeing how each one of them steeled herself against what came in the wake of Julian's death. That small gesture, so seemingly harmless, had its own message — about protection and denial and the messy lamina of themselves that everyone carried.

Finally, Sloane thought that Mary exactly knew how much she could do by neatly wiping. It was an unobtrusive attempt to save her dignity, conceal her weakness and defend herself — not least from her own guilt. The small things that tend to be overlooked were indicative of fears lurking beneath the surface. For me, cleaning that glass was not just about getting everything to be clear; it was also about fighting off chaos and thinking in a clear way. Sloane understood that in there everyone has their own means of protecting themselves. She also learnt that even tiny efforts can make a big difference.

She wiped again, and the sluggish dance of her hand intensified as a mild tremor rippled through her fingers. The dance was muted and deliberate, almost meditative. But there was a jittery quality to it, as if something were being said but not said. Sloane noticed how the small signals — the way her eyes flicked to and fro, how she clamped her jaw — gave it away that inside, perhaps every time Ms Palin mustered herself to answer or laugh, her mind was racing to keep secrets that would ruin everything she said she valued. It wasn't only the glass she kept clear: it was her world, free from anything that might have been – well, uncomfortable." It was like each swipe did more than just remove fingerprints. It was to shield her from the tempest raging within her and help her keep her presence of mind should there be a revelation.

Mary's work was also a silent way of battling the guilt that could swamp her life, an unconscious way of keeping some distance between herself and her doubt. Her every motion was a thready layer between her and the truth she didn't want to confront. Perhaps, she had reasoned, by controlling her environment—by washing the glass constantly—she could control her terror. It was a fragile shield, and one that would easily be broken if jostled, but she clung to it tenaciously. This little habit provided Mary with just enough firm footing to stay where she was when all the questions about Julian's decline, her part in it and whether or not her own secrets would find light were whirling through her mind. Wiping at that point was a quiet act of resistance for her, a measure to keep safe an already shattered truth.

The move revealed another side of Sloane's personality

— how far she would go to defend herself, her reputation or her secrets. There was that little, repeated motion with the hand, and it told a story of someone caught in between telling the truth and protecting herself, trying to keep her inner turmoil cased behind a serene face. When people behave in this sort of way, it is generally an indictment more eloquent than a confession, and Mary was fighting her private battles there in that silent pride of mastery. The wiping was gentle, but the effects were great, demonstrating how small things can cloak big problems. Sloane learnt that sometimes watching those small, insignificant movements could tell you more about a person — what they were trying to conceal or protect at all costs.

Ultimately, that act of wiping the glass down was a quiet but forceful symbol of the greater struggle each woman wrestled with: whether to confront their fears or continue to keep them at arm's length. In a universe of tales and secrets, even the subtlest gestures can reveal their hidden connotations. Each act is a kind of silent language of self-defence.

However, the absence of Mila Novak is an awful vacuum where her final moments and the tension of her escape remain suspended in time. It's a clue to the storm inside her thoughts. The guilt is so heavy, in fact, that the air feels thick and dense. She is a ghost in the room, and the whispers of her impulsive decisions linger long after her footsteps have ceased. The moments she left you with stay in your mind like an annoying song, making you wonder and feel all over the place.

The circumstances surrounding her departure speak volumes in their own right. The room is cooler now, as if when her presence heated it up and she left, all that was keeping warm became cold again. The faint odour of stale coffee wafts through the air, a bitter vestige of former times. There are little indications that she was in a hurry here: A chair was pushed back from the table; pages of her manuscript were out and unread as well as half-read, so it is almost as if she quit reading mid-line (did something alarm her into flight?). Everything feels wrong, bent and filled with the unexpressed.

The gentle tick-tock of the clock fills the silence, reminding her he's not there second by second. It's not just her body that is missing; it's the spirit and essence for which she was a vehicle, filling the room with ideas full of life and arguments full of heat. Of shadows, nothing is left. As she exits, there is tension in the room just because everyone can see the way that she leaves. It's as if the walls can hear her fears and regrets while she is on the brink of a nervous breakdown.

It's as if the room is caught in time, like it's just that moment after she left. The calamity she left behind is in stark contrast to the calm that now prevails. It is her frenzied escape that becomes the point of origin – not just what she was running from, but now also vengeance for her having been chased out. The coffee cup is overturned, and a brown liquid spills all over it, as if mirroring the black thoughts inside of her. It paints a vivid picture of what's gone wrong — a vivid picture of her inner turmoil swaddled in guilt and pain.

By the side of the bed stood Detective Byrne, looking silently down on it — fixing her gaze on a glass that stood there empty; she was too clean to have been bothered by anyone. Its surface held no smudges, no fingerprints; it carried nothing but the shining cleanliness of something wiped clean, as if it had been manipulated into an empty space. There was a metallic-tinged smell of disinfectant in the air, but underneath it stood something else, colder and more ineffable. The room had a presence which exercised beautiful feet and was dimmed by the tranquillity of the appearance. Byrne's fingers itched to snatch at the glass and chase after the lost trail that lay somewhere under its smooth skin. It was the one nugget of truth that had been scrubbed on purpose.

She looked at Mary, just a few paces away, and the gravity of the moment settled between them. From the outside, Mary's face appeared as it always did, but there was a flicker there — they could tell by the tiny twitch at the corner of her mouth and a hesitation in her eyes that meant she was lying.

"The glass," Byrne said, quietly but deliberately. "It's been cleaned up. Did you not expect me to notice?"

Mary pressed her lips together, and doubt flickered across the shadow of her face for an instant. So she steadied herself and her voice and spoke:

"I never touched that glass," she said in a level voice that seemed somehow rehearsed.

Instead of making eye contact with Byrne, she seemed to be concealing something beneath polished denial.

"I don't know why it looks so clean... perhaps someone was in here before you came."

The air around them seemed to shrink; it was heavy with unspoken stuff. Byrne didn't ask right away because she could sense that Mary was teetering on a tightrope between defence and something more fragile: a denial that felt like there was information she wasn't yet willing to share.

CHAPTER SIX

THE LAPTOP

Mary sat at her desk with her fingers lightly resting on the cold surface of her laptop. She often forgot how quiet it was in her office those early mornings, with the hum of the building outside being a distant sound. Today, her mind wandered away from work and focused on the little things that were less important than she thought, like what to make for dinner and the meeting she had forgotten. She absentmindedly scrolled through emails on the screen, barely registering what she saw. As she saw a message highlighted in her inbox, her gaze slowed. She recognised it right away from the subject line, but she still ignored it. It was there, unopened, a quiet annoyance hiding in plain sight among more boring messages. She didn't feel the tension in her chest break; she just didn't notice. The email was about Julian's death and the details that could change everything. But she kept staring at the flickering screen, not knowing that her silence was hiding an important truth.

As time went on, her mind drifted further away from the blinking cursor and the message she hadn't read. Her shallow breaths were the only thing that broke the silence in the room. Each one felt faster than the last. She was lost in thoughts about Julian—his smile when they first met, the way his eyes seemed to hold secrets she would never fully understand. She grabbed her tea, took a sip, and then looked back at the computer with a blank stare. The soft glow of the laptop lit up her face and made shadows that moved across it. But in that quiet moment, she had no idea how important that unopened email was. The notification badge stayed the same, a clear sign of her neglect from afar. There was something going on that she didn't know about, a truth hidden in a text she never bothered to open. She might have found the answer to questions she hadn't asked yet in that message, but she just didn't see it.

The office was filled with the faint scent of stale coffee and old paper, underscoring the stillness that enveloped her. The light from her screen flickered and made the messy desk, which was covered in papers and notebooks, look spooky. The city noise from outside came in softly, like the honking of cars and the footsteps of people walking by late at night. Mary didn't notice all of these details because she was too busy with her thoughts. Her hand hovered over the keyboard, and she looked unsure, but she chose to ignore the email again. She might have thought it was just another work-related thing, or she might have known deep down that it was better not to see it. No matter what, she didn't realise that the silence she was feeling wasn't just her peace; it was also her silence about a message that could have explained everything—Julian's last hours and the truth she didn't see. The email sat there, unopened, waiting for her to open it. It held secrets that could change everything she thought she knew about what had happened.

Sloane entered the room, and her heart raced as she saw the mess of scribbled-upon papers, spilt coffee cups, and some half-finished books thrown everywhere in what had become a makeshift study over the past weeks. The air was heavy and dense, with that eerie hush. They fell on the laptop she had left open last night, a taunting little cursor blinking ominously at her. It was all just a specific type of discourse, an ordinary day gone top-sy-turvy, and yet everything seemed so very wrong. She could feel the tension swaddling her like a cloak, weighing on her chest.

When Mila's gone, it becomes more significant than just someone missing. She's not physically present where the investigation is taking place in the small, darkened room, but her presence seems to stand there in the absence of sound. It's as if the space she should be in is pulled taut and thin with unsaid tension that no one is willing to fill. The others—Mary, Sloane and Byrne—glance around the table past the chair in which Mila should be sitting. The missing is not merely a sign of absence but of emotional exile. Mila has run, and she's running away from more than the scene before her eyes; she is fleeing the gravity of what has occurred, the knotted mass of questions that threaten to ensnare her.

Her lack of a presence is a clue, a tip-off that all is not well in the relationships that bind these characters to one another. She is the mistress, the enigmatic figure entangled in truth and untruth, guilt and denial. No one knows exactly where Mila is — or what she's telling herself when the lights are out, in that dim corner where she prefers to sequester herself. The murkiness invites wild theories, but what's heard from outside of the window is silence other than the sound of cars far away. The fact that she is gone in the hour so critical to her makes it feel as though we have an incomplete investigation, a story missing an important sentence. Yet within this vacancy is a deafening admission that unsettles the delicate equilibrium maintained by the women who are left.

It's cold in the room now, a chill of unanswered questions. Cracks of doubt begin to crack the polished surfaces, as all of those thoughts about what Mila is getting up to and why bubble just below the surface. Although she's not here, every item indicates her mental state: the hasty erasure of missives, a faint aroma of perfume left in a chair cushion, the negligent loss of a hairpin — all are preserved as if caught in amber in this fraction before she comes back or vanishes for good. There are actual scenes of Laura Palmer; her being there in the first scene turns every frame into a silent attempt to find her. It's like the heart of the mystery is beating on hold, waiting for Mila to return or maybe fade away altogether.

The time around the laptop crackles with a quiet charge. It sits on the table like a dormant witness, the keyboard slightly dusty, its screen dark save for a faint glow around the edges to indicate recent use. Fingers are hesitant over the keys, and doubt hangs thick in the air. The laptop contains secrets no one can yet fathom — a digital repository of memories, lies and half-truths that may further thwart everyone. The room appears to contract, the pressure of anticipation bearing down with the sense that the device possesses its own respiration, throbbing with the capacity to reveal what all want hidden or need desperately to prove.

Lap", (intervening), "Day Dreamin'. They were playing solitaire / that game nobody can deal so well, roulette, and twenty-one." --_---_-- The hum of the laptop fills the silence but for an old clock on the wall ticking something. It's almost a code: the idleness, the slow unwinding of time next to the unread stories imprisoned in those files. Even the air tastes of metal, as if you could cut it, add a little salt and eat it. The laptop may contain a voice recording, deleted emails, or the final draft of a manuscript — anything that would disrupt the troubled equilibrium between suspicion and certainty. Eyes dart between the screen and the play of the shadows on my bedroom wall, hoping to catch any tiny tell-tale sign that might appear when the screen eventually sparks into life.

Everything gets charged with meaning in the simplest way here. One of them was a curling sticky note, half-blurred with almost-erased scribbling. The name of a little-known file blinking in one corner of the screen's taskbar. These little threads weave a tapestry, prompting you to look closer and not giving away easy answers. Each click, each pause, pulls the knot tighter and tighter. It has the flavour of static before a storm, heavy with unspoken fears and the breathless hope that what waits inside might warp free the tangled truth —

or complicate the mystery anew.

And while its owner hesitates, the people in the room feel a tug toward everything they cannot see. Truth isn't exhibited here, but it murmurs over at the edges, willing to rise whenever someone has the courage to unlock what Mila left behind. This silence is charged, and the mounting tension now isn't just about the device itself but also a metaphor: all four lives snared in Julian's last act, waiting to see who will crack first under pressure from this medallion of secrets.

In such situations, where crucial evidence sits locked behind a screen, patience is as important/telling as curiosity. Time to wait for just the right time to reveal what's kept hidden allows for truth to be seen with open eyes and not in hasty reaction. Sometimes silence and absence say more than words, and knowing when not to speak may be the most revealing clue of all.

Byrne bent over Julian's messy desk, her fingers just above the keyboard. The room smelt like old paper and stale coffee, and it was quiet, like when something awful happens. As she looked through Julian's laptop, she saw something strange: the trash folder was full, and in it was a deleted email, along with broken drafts and other junk. It looked as if it hadn't been touched, like a ghost waiting to be found. Byrne clicked on the bin and paused when the email with the subject line "Urgent: Contract Termination" showed up. The words were simple to understand, but they had a lot of meaning. Julian's name was at the top, and the address of the sender was spelt wrong, which made it look like they were in a hurry to send it. The message was short, almost rude:

```
"This is to let you know that we are
ending our contract right away. We
can't keep working together because
of what happened recently."
```

The email, which was no longer in the inbox, hinted at a tense split with the publisher, something Julian was hiding behind his calm public demeanour. Byrne stared at it, knowing that this could help him figure out what Julian was hiding. It suggested that Julian had a problem that he hadn't fully faced before he died, one that might have made him more hopeless than anyone knew.

Byrne called on Sloane into her office a few days later. The tension in the air was thick. Sloane, who is usually calm and sharp, looked pale and distracted, as if she had a weight on her shoulders that she couldn't hide. Byrne's voice was steady but sharp:

"I found that email. The one you got rid of after Julian died."

She saw Sloane's face tighten and a flash of guilt cross her eyes. Byrne went on, "This wasn't because the publisher was pressuring or because Julian's last book didn't do well. There was something else, something deeper."

"Julian was having a hard time," Sloane said after a long pause. "Yes, he was in a lot of pain, but he wasn't going to kill himself. That's what everyone believes."

Byrne nodded slowly, knowing that the truth was more complicated than anyone thought.

'This is how Julian wanted it to end. He didn't kill himself because he was unhappy with his job or health. He made it look like he had failed so that the world would have to see him on his own terms. His death was his last great move, a planned act based on a feeling of loss that went beyond money or art. Julian was tired of being let down, and he knew that his best days were behind him. He used his words—his death—to send a message that no one could ignore.'

Sloane turned away and was quiet, carrying the weight of her silence. Byrne got it: Julian's death wasn't about tragedy or pressure; it was about a man finally accepting that he couldn't fix his fading genius and the personal ruin that came with it.

CHAPTER SEVEN

THE "OTHER WOMAN"

Mary West seems calm and sure of herself in the room where she is being questioned. She has great posture, and all of her muscles are calm but ready. Detective Byrne's piercing eyes are on her, looking for any sign of the trouble that is brewing just beyond her serene surface. Mary stays calm and controlled as she answers questions regarding Mila Novak, Julian's protégé, even though the air is heated. When she talks, there is a very slight hint of doubt in her eyes, but the serene cardiologist immediately hides it beneath her practice mask. She looks calm on the outside, but inside her head is a tempest of thoughts, many of which are about Julian and Mila and are full of unspoken struggle.

Mary remarks: "Mila is a great artist."

Her voice is calm, and she doesn't exhibit any evidence that she's getting angry. For years now, she has been working closely with Julian. They were quite close. She says the words without any trouble, but the way she delivers them makes it sound like something else is going on. Mary remembers Mila's youthful ambition, which made her anxious since it was so raw. But she hides her envy well, even if it makes her throat hard every time she talks. She examines the detective's face every time she talks about Mila to see how much power the truth could offer her and how much it would cost.

Sloane Porter never quite understood what Mila Novak meant to her, but she knew that Julian Vane was very close to the younger lady. Sloane felt nervous when she watched Mila gliding softly around the outskirts of their shared universe, like a shadow that was just out of reach. She never directly challenged Mila, and she didn't know what texts or papers Mila had taken. Instead, she felt the weight of an unknown menace, like an invisible hand ripping up the finely balanced story she had worked so hard to weave around Julian's legacy.

Mila seemed to be both an insider and an outsider. She was talented, determined, and dangerous in ways that Sloane couldn't yet put into words. Sloane was wary because she didn't know what would happen, so she kept away, only letting professional etiquette get in the way. Every talk was planned out. She didn't want to start a conflict over words or secrets, but the idea of Mila having any control over Julian's last story made her nervous.

Sloane knew she was working in the dark, putting together bits of information and clues that showed Mila was more than simply a fan of the book; she might have the keys to his last and deepest truths. There were times when Sloane watched Mila very intently, looking at her face, timing, and even the books she was carrying. None of it gave the full picture, but each bit of knowledge added to the web of possibilities: Was Mila trying to change the truth or keep it hidden? Were the writings she possessed proof that Julian's meticulously created universe was full of holes, or was there a fresh story ready to be told?

Even though Julian's death threw a long and confusing shadow over everyone, the questions stayed heavy and unaddressed. Sloane had a lot of different feelings about Mila that she didn't tell anyone about. She knew Mila as Julian's student, lover, and muse, and she couldn't stop thinking about how she was a part of the last chapter of his life. There was obviously jealousy, but there was also something deeper: a need to defend Julian's legacy, which was weak and coming apart and threatened by the things Mila may do that no one knew about.

Sloane recognised that Mila's desire was hazardous, but she also viewed her as a fearful woman trying to take control of a situation that had gotten out of hand. Sloane couldn't stop thinking about how Mila's actions, whether deliberate or not, may undermine all the work that had gone into making Julian's death look a certain way. She had been creating a story for years that would retain Julian's place in the literary world, even as his health, reputation, and inventiveness waned. Mila's presence now brought up feelings that were hard to foresee, like remorse, desperation, or even regret.

These soft murmurs made Sloane want to defend Julian's memory and her own life, even when it meant going against what was truly happening. Sloane acted like she was in charge, but she knew there was a fear deep inside. It's not only that Mila has sensitive texts; it's also what those texts might show the world and how they could affect the balance of power. If Mila knew the tale Julian wanted to keep secret, if she wanted to modify the way he died or disclose the truth behind the myth, then Sloane's carefully controlled world could break apart. Sloane stayed quiet but kept her eye on Mila from a distance. There was a lot of scepticism, rage, and unwilling respect in her head.

The first time Mila saw the message pop up on her phone, more than a year ago, her stomach dropped and muscles tensed. There was a simple, unpretentious text message on the screen: ***Tonight, see you there. Important.***

It was not extraordinary for Julian to send her late-night messages, but there was something about this one that felt different. The mild tremble of her fingers as she unlocked her phone revealed the combination of anticipation and unease. She looked at the words, a million questions breezing through her mind, but also a flutter of excitement — because perhaps she would get to see him, connect with the man who had become something of a secret for her, some kind of refuge from the world.

She felt the rush of the missive instantly, a small shiver as her heart began to race. She had a bubbling kernel of hope, thinking just maybe, something would be different on this night. But beneath that thrill was a twinge of concern. Julian had been unpredictable lately and secretive in a way that was frustrating to her. Was this simply a harmless flirtation, or was there something more to it: an edge she wasn't quite ready to experience? Now the fear whispered in unvoiced, which is unsettling. Then this meeting had devolved into madness. What if whatever she was hiding could be exposed, ruining everything she wanted to save? The danger crackled along her skin, real and sharp, even as she yearned to leap toward the possibility that waited at the other end of that message.

When you follow your instincts, you must act quickly. She paused for only a second before reaching for her coat, and the coarse coat scratched at her fingers as she pulled it on over herself. Her phone buzzed anew —

another fast alert, a prompt or possibly a word of caution. In her head she pictured the worst-case scenarios playing out. But her body, trapped in a tug of war between dread and longing, propelled her forward. The rain took long moments to reach the pavement, and as it did, CS Gas that had been expelled from the sky filled our lungs with its ghastly taste. Pushing open her door and stepping out into the dark, she felt alive in a way that she hadn't for days. Each footstep thunked down heavily, weighty with intent; each ba-dunk drummed in her ears.

The streetlights painted thin, swaying pools of light on the damp pavement. The cold air was crisp and clean, filling her lungs with each gulp. Her shoes whispered and squeaked as she moved quickly, eyes sweeping back and forth. Would she see him? Would this be a moment that undid everything or brought everything into focus? She was clammy-handed now and curling her fingers into fists to keep her focus amid the thudding in her chest. The night shadows appeared to elongate like dark fingers writhing across the dirt toward her, and she felt the tenuous line between thrill and terror was easy to step over. Still, she moved forward, propelled by that odd tug of hope and foreboding, so desperate to learn what their night would yield.

When Mila at last came to where he had told her to stop—a silent alley behind the derelict bookshop—she was alert. She smelt something mordant, like tobacco and some metallic smell, a warning signal perhaps. She shivered and glanced about, eyes scanning over each shadowy shift. Moments were stretching long, a slow drag of anticipation that made her breasts tighten and her stomach as well. Then a shadow moved around the corner, and she gasped. Her painfully pounding heart seemed to stop for a breath as she waited for him to lurch forward—or the havoc to start. This rush of adrenaline, combined with her fear, reminded her just how much she longed for answers and just how linked she was to the danger that lay obscured. Her heart was racing; she had no idea what would come next, and each second seemed to stretch out impossibly long.

At last Julian's angular shape came out of shadows. Only half his face was visible in the dim light. The moment was electric, a headlong rush of hope and apprehension. Mila's nerves eased a small bit but never quite went away as they muttered rushed words back and forth. In the conflict her body was betraying that wanting to trust him, and this crawling doubt maybe she really didn't understand what was happening there or why she was there. Every look, every whisper was significant. She found herself running through the argument again in her mind: outbursts, furtive suspicion and violent feelings that she was about to tip over into something perilous. In that silence, punctuated by the fast pounding of her heartbeat and low whooshing sound of wind, Mila became aware that her precarious equilibrium was dangling on a taut rope stretched between excitement and dread, with the understanding that tonight would either finish tearing apart or knotting together everything she'd believed true about Julian's past, herself and what had really happened.

And yet, now and then as she stood in that discovered grimy hole, Mila wondered whether the price of information was worth it. Was she ready to face the truth, or did her fear really fit better under a banner of wanting more? There was something uncertain about the taste of the night air. The shadows flickered once more, nearer, and she found her hand resting on the pocket of her dress as it gripped onto the corner of her shawl. Her entire form was alive with tremors of expectancy and with fear. One thing was certain—the path of her destiny and maybe Julian's would be forever altered after she took that next step into the unknown. That is the bizarre thing about fears related to secrets: they breed beneath the surface and simply lie in wait, waiting for the time when they emerge, prepared to overwhelm anything standing in their way. And Mila knew, somehow, she was really near that moment then.

Detective Byrne sat at her desk and read Julian's last few text messages. Each line was like a piece of a puzzle that indicated more than just what he said; it illustrated how he lived his dying days. The texts indicated a deep melancholy and a sense of hopelessness that made many question his connections. But one message stuck out as weird and fragmented, which made it seem like someone might have tried to poison someone. She was horrified not just by what Julian wrote but also by the inexplicable quiet from his wife, Mary.

Mary was typically serene, a rock in the middle of Julian's tumultuous life. But now, she seemed much more suspicious because she wasn't talking. Is it possible that she was hiding something because she didn't say anything? Byrne had more and more questions as she glanced at the screen. A voice whispered what could happen: Was Mary responsible for Julian's death?

Byrne moved her head to look at the notes on her desk. They were about Mary's job as a heart doctor and the strange things people were saying about their marriage. They had been good friends and respected each other, but Julian's life had gotten worse in both his personal and professional life. Did Mary think she was stuck because of his problems? She leaned back in her chair and couldn't help but feel the tension in the air, like an unseen ghost that was there in every word and every pause.

The investigation fell apart like a ball of yarn that

wouldn't come apart, with each pull revealing more lies. Byrne couldn't get over the notion that Mary was hiding more than simply her misery. It looked like she was performing or practising something because of how she was acting. Mary was able to alter the subject every time Byrne pushed her for further information about the day Julian died. It was upsetting, and it made Byrne question everything she thought she knew about their immaculate front.

Mila, Julian's girlfriend, came out of nowhere and made the story even more confusing. The more Byrne knew about Mila, the more questions she had for herself. Mila was brilliant and determined, but her relationship with Julian seemed to be crumbling apart. There were stories about their passionate meetings, but there was also a violent argument that caused an accident that may have killed someone.

Byrne needed to formulate a plan. She needed to know not just what had happened but also why everyone was so desperate to keep their secrets. If she could only untie the threads that bound them together, she might finally be able to see the full image. Byrne kept a list of items that linked Mary, Sloane, and Mila, the three ladies who were being looked into. All three had reasons that were easy to hide. There were feelings, money difficulties, and personal aspirations involved, all of which wove a hazardous web of betrayal that made Byrne question her instincts. Who was actually telling the truth, and more crucially, whose lies would finally show them?

PART II

THE DAY BEFORE

Chapter Eight

The Morning Argument

(9:00 AM)

The harsh, clinical light in the kitchen made everything sharper: the cold counters, the faint smear of jam on the table, and the smell of burnt toast that filled the warm morning air. She held the small white bottle tightly in one hand. Her voice was steady, but there was some-thing tense underneath it.

"Julian, take your medicine."

She spoke the words with a controlled calmness, but her eyes showed the growing tension as they darted to his pale, drawn face and then back to the bottle. The faint smell of burnt bread and the faint smell of medicine, which was bitter and sterile, hung between them like a promise that was too strong to keep. This morning, the kitchen was their battlefield, and Mary was both a soldier and a peacekeeper.

Julian sat still in his chair, staring out the window as if the outside world could help him get away from what was happening inside. The early sun made long, shaky shadows on his thin cheekbones, but his eyes were cold and still.

He said, "I don't need it," without turning around.

The words were sharp but quiet, as if they were final. Mary's calmness was starting to fade as he refused. The only sound breaking the heavy silence was the soft click of the spoon against the porcelain bowl. At that moment, they were worlds apart. She was weighed down by the knowledge of his decline and the strong desire to keep control. He was clinging stubbornly to his pride and hiding behind walls that Mary knew all too well.

She could see the space between them getting bigger, like ice spreading over still water. Julian's cold refusal wasn't just about the pills. It was about everything she couldn't touch: the illness creeping into his bones and the slow unravelling that scared her more than anything else. Mary's grip on the bottle got tighter.

"You promised," she said softly, her voice almost breaking. "You said you would take care of yourself."

The unspoken words made the room feel smaller, with those promises now broken rather than kept. Julian's silence was enough of an answer; it was a protective refusal that sounded like giving up.

She moved closer, and the edge of the worn table brushed against the fabric of her blouse. The smell of perfumed soap from her morning routine lingered on her skin. The air was thick, sharp, and difficult to breathe all at once. She added, "The doctor said you need it," with a quiet insistence that broke the silence. But Julian's eyes stayed on the grey sky outside the glass, which was far away and closed off, keeping her out. There was more to that stillness than just defiance or stubbornness. It was a silent declaration of control in a body that no longer obeyed.

Mary's breath caught when she saw the pill bottle and the crumpled label in her hand. She thought about how they had gotten to this point, with the slow, steady unravelling that had happened over the years. She remembered the quiet days when Julian's hand shook just enough for her to notice, the pressure building behind his eyes, and the private wars he fought between the man he was and the man he used to be. She thought about the medical records she had hidden away in her office, the doses she had double-checked, and the nights she had stayed up charting his symptoms. She was a healer and a professional, but in this kitchen, where Julian wouldn't take his meds, she felt helpless in a way that no stethoscope could fix.

There was a smell of burnt toast and something else, something colder and unspoken. It was the sharp edge of fear, mixed with tiredness. Mary knew that this fight in the kitchen wasn't the first, and it wouldn't be the last. But every time she said no, it felt like a brick in the wall that was growing between them, an invisible line that could break everything she had worked so hard to keep together.

"Just a few more days," she whispered, and the plea hung in the stale air.

Julian didn't say anything. He moved in his chair, but the only sound was the faint scrape of leather on tile.

At that moment, the quiet tension and the clash of despair and hope became a fragile heartbeat in their complicated lives. Mary knew this was about more than just pills. It was a fight for freedom, respect, and the right to choose how to die. And in the dim light of the kitchen, with the smell of burnt toast and bitter medicine still in the air, they stood on opposite sides of a fragile fault line, neither ready to cross it.

When Sloane picked up the phone, Julian's voice was shaky and broken. It was as if he had to pull the words out of his throat with a lot of effort, and each syllable shook with anger and sadness. He sounded like he was in a lot of trouble and couldn't get out of the fog of exhaustion that was making him feel like he was drowning. He said her name with such raw urgency that it made her stomach tighten. He could tell that something was breaking inside him, and he needed her to know exactly how much she was suffocating him and how difficult life had become lately.

He began to ramble right away, with words coming out faster than he could control.

"I can't keep doing this," he said in a whisper. "Every

day gets worse. The stress and expectations make me feel like I'm stuck in my head and can't breathe. Sloane, it's killing me to turn every word and line into a work of art. I swear I can't keep living like this."

His voice broke again, and it got thicker with feeling. He stopped for a moment and then said:

"She's watching me, every move I make, and I don't see a way out. This noise is making me lose myself. I need you to know how awful things have gotten."

It wasn't just a request for help; it was a cry from someone who was stuck in a spiral they couldn't get out of.

Sloane listened without saying anything, and with each passing second, her fingers tightened around her phone. The sounds of the city or the muffled hum of her office faded away as she listened to only his voice. The thing that stood out to her the most was how broken it sounded, like someone was falling apart. She felt her heart tighten because she knew Julian had always been weak on the inside. Hearing his voice this way made her realise how far gone he was. She wanted to reach through the queue and grab him and tell him to hang on, but she didn't know what he really needed, so words didn't seem to work.

As Julian's words hung in the air, she felt the weight of his confession settle like a stone in her stomach. She knew right away that this call was a turning point and that whatever was going on was worse than a normal problem. His voice sounded frustrated, which made me think he felt like he had lost something and that his life was becoming a cage that was getting tighter every day. She thought about what she could do for a moment. Was this just another step in his downward spiral, or could she reach out and hold him back?

A long silence hung between them, filled with unspoken fears. Finally, Julian whispered:

"I just... I can't go on like this. I don't know how much longer I can fight because she's ruining everything."

She couldn't stop her mind from racing as she tried to figure out if this was a real moment of despair or just more manipulation from someone who had always played with words and truths. But she knew enough, having worked with Julian for years, that this was different. He was exhausted and had a raw edge to his voice. He couldn't take it anymore.

She clenched her teeth and felt the helplessness come over her. She knew that whatever happened next would change everything. She could only listen, hold on to those words, and get ready for what would happen in the next few tense hours of the morning's chaos.

Mila could hardly breathe as she clicked through her messages. The familiar sound of her phone ringing made her mind even more chaotic. Every text from Julian felt like a knife stabbing her heart. He had written, "I know something's wrong." That one line kept going through her mind, with a creepy undertone that wouldn't go away. What did he mean by that? Every word seemed to have a hidden meaning that made fun of her innocence.

As she frantically scrolled up, her thumb stopped over another text. The timestamp showed that it had come in right after their last heated conversation. He had warned that you wouldn't be able to get away with this. What did he think she was trying to get away from? These new messages felt like a storm was about to break, in contrast to the sweet memories of their first days together. She felt a wave of anger, confusion, and a sense of doom coming over her.

The blue light from her phone lit up her face and showed that she was sweating. She dug her nails into her palms to ground herself as she tried to figure out what it all meant. Did he really think she would hurt him? Panic rose in her throat, making it hard for her to breathe. How could he come to that conclusion? She felt trapped, and a sneaky thought crept in: What if he really thought she could do something so horrible? Was he putting her to the test? She felt weak and exposed after reading his last text, which sounded almost like a taunt. She looked at the screen, daring it to tell her the truth she so badly wanted to know. She knew, though, that the more she dug, the more tangled the web became.

The morning light fell unevenly on Byrne's messy desk, creating long shadows that covered the papers and devices that were all over the place in front of her. The half-closed blinds let in a little bit of the city's quiet hum, but inside the small precinct office, the air was so still that time seemed to stand still.

Byrne leaned in and followed the patterns on Julian Vane's phone records with her eyes. Every call and text felt like a thread in a complicated web that he had to untangle before the truth got even further away. The numbers, the times, and even the short breaks between conversations all hinted at something deeper, something hidden beneath the surface of everyday life.

The calls had a strange pattern. Julian called a few numbers over and over again. Some calls were made late at night, some were made quickly after each other, and some were left unanswered, like unanswered questions. Byrne's fingers slowly tapped on the table as she listened to parts of voicemails saved on his phone. The voices were tense, anxious, or carefully hidden. It was clear that Julian wasn't just a fading novelist who was having a hard time with the passage of time. Underneath it all, he was a man fighting his fears and stuck in a maze of control and avoidance. Byrne could almost feel the quiet dread that Julian must have felt. It was the kind of fear that doesn't explode outward but instead curls inward, changing everything it touches.

Byrne saw that some numbers were often linked to Julian's wife, Mary. The calls were short and sometimes rude, and when you heard them on speaker, the tone changed slightly. Julian felt like he was walking on a tightrope, trying to keep things in order but always worried about what might go wrong. Other contacts sent longer, more secretive messages that hinted at secrets that should not be shared. Byrne's stomach turned at the thought that Julian might not have been the victim of a sudden tragedy but instead a prisoner of his own making, tied up in a complicated relationship with his wife that made him feel both safe and scared at the same time.

As Byrne went through this digital trail, the tension in the room seemed to grow without anyone saying anything. She wondered if Julian's repeated calls to his wife were because he really trusted her or because he was trying to change the story that everyone else believed. Was Julian just scared of Mary, or was he also scared of what might happen if the truth came out? Byrne could tell that the lines between victim and puppeteer were getting blurry. Every call and message could have been carefully planned to shape how people thought about Julian's last days, keeping them in a story that wasn't quite real. The detective's eyes narrowed as she tried to figure out which times Julian was petrified and which times he was just acting to keep power in Julian's hands even after he died.

Byrne's anxiety grew as she followed the digital trail deeper, wondering if the man's fear was a reflection of his own inner demons. Was Julian frightened of the wife he depended on, or was he the one controlling the people closest to him, like his agent, his lover, and everyone else? The phone logs didn't give a clear answer, but they did show that the person had lived a careful life in the shadows. Byrne thought about the conversations that Julian and Mary had, which were full of unspoken threats or hidden confessions. The truth seemed to be getting harder to find by the minute, caught up in layers of guilt, desperation, and control. Byrne felt the weight of a deliberately hidden story with each thread she unravelled. This made her look more closely at the small, telling details that were right in front of her.

By the time Byrne got up from the desk, the sun was higher and the light in the room was harsher, but the picture was still blurry. Julian's phone was more than just a phone; it was a silent witness to a man torn apart by his conflicting needs: the desire to be understood, the need to control the story of his own life, and a quiet fear of the woman next to him. Byrne knew that getting to the bottom of those calls was the key to finding out what really happened in the last hours. But the question that kept bothering her was simple and cold: was Julian scared because he had lost control, or was he the one pulling the strings, putting on a final show that would keep everyone guessing? Byrne had to go deeper into the digital maze to get closer to the answer. She couldn't trust anything at face value and had to pay attention to what the silence between calls might reveal.

CHAPTER NINE

THE PUBLISHER

(10:00 AM)

Mary stood still in the dark room, staring at the cracked plaster on the wall across from her. The place was so quiet that the only sounds were the faint hum of the city outside and the soft sound of her breathing. She didn't move or blink, as if looking at something could somehow stop what was happening inside her. Her mind kept going over the call Julian had just made. His voice sounded distant, robotic, and almost as if it belonged to someone else. That call had changed everything, but now all she could feel was the weight of it pressing down on her, heavy and unrelenting, keeping her in place without a word or protest. The walls of the room seemed to close in on her, trapping her in her silence.

Julian was slumped in his chair across the room, and he looked so tired that his face looked like it was made of paper. His eyes, which used to be sharp and full of life, now stared into space. His face looked empty, like a shell that had been emptied overnight. His face showed no emotion: no anger, no regret, no hope. Just the empty face of someone who was lost in the huge, sterile silence that surrounded him. It was like his mind had gone to a quiet, cold place far away from this room. His body conveyed the narrative of exhaustion, battles fought and lost, and a diminishing spark that seemed unlikely to return. Still, there was an unsettling feeling that he was waiting for something, or maybe he had already decided it was time to leave it all behind.

Julian's face stayed blank in the silence that followed, with no sign of thought or feeling. His hands were limp on his lap and shook just a little, showing that he was tense, but no one else seemed to notice. His shoes softly scraped against the wooden floor as he moved, almost without thinking. His eyes finally moved to the wall, but they didn't stay there. It was like they weren't seeing or taking in anything. Every breath he took was shallow and quick, like a reminder that life was still slipping away in slow, unavoidable steps. The air in the room was thick with the smell of dust, old paper, and the faint scent of his cologne, which was all that was left of a man who used to live for words and stories but now just lived in this endless, pointless silence.

A car passing by in the distance briefly broke the silence,

but neither of them left their worlds. Julian's mind was racing, caught between memories and a strange numbness that made everything outside seem far away and unreal. His face looked emptier than before, as if the call had taken all the life out of it. He looked at the wall again, not to find comfort but maybe to see through it, past the surface. He looked blank but focused, as if he were looking for something he knew he would never find. Time seemed to stretch in that quiet moment, filling the space between his last breath and whatever came next. Julian was barely there in this room; he was just a shell that held the echoes of a mind that was already broken.

Sloane sat in her dark office, staring at her phone as it vibrated angrily on the desk. The call from the publisher made her already frayed nerves feel like they were going to break. She couldn't stop hearing their words, which were like a drumbeat of disappointment. They said they were letting him go, and she could feel each word eating away at her calm demeanour. Julian, the outstanding novelist she had supported for years, was about to become a literary ghost, and the weight of that truth was heavy on her chest. As her heart raced, she went over the conversation again and again, each insistent tone cutting deeper into her mind and threatening to show the cracks in her carefully crafted professionalism.

The call seemed to last forever, with each second feeling like an eternity. They kept asking her questions and trying to get her to promise that Julian's decline wouldn't hurt her reputation. Sloane felt the weight of their doubts and disbelief when she told them that Julian was just going through a rough patch. She tried to sound sure of herself, but all she could think about was how each word she spoke sounded like air whistling through a broken dam. The call finally ended, but the effects stayed with her, ringing in her ears like an annoying echo. The harsh truth was that she had to face the ugly truth: Julian's career was falling apart, and they were both headed for trouble.

Sloane picked up her phone again after the call because she felt like she had to talk to Julian. She hovered her fingers over the screen and paused, not sure what words could close the gap that had grown between them. When she finally called, there was only silence after he hung up on her. It was as if he had entered a different world, leaving her behind on the threshold. She felt empty inside, like there was nothing where there used to be a connection.

Julian had always been difficult to deal with, but this time alone felt worse than ever. There was a lot of tension in the air between them that they didn't say anything about. She couldn't help but think back to the things that led to this break: his distant looks, his late-night absences, and the slow, creeping despair that changed his once lively personality. He had learnt how to be detached, shutting himself off from the world with layers of bitterness and cynicism.

Sloane felt like something important had come to an end when she heard the phone click off. She had put her heart and soul into keeping it alive. Every second that went by without an answer made her more and more aware that she might not be able to save him this time. She remembered the dreams they used to have about literary success and praise. Now, those dreams looked like ghosts of what they had once wanted. The troubled artist had turned into a ghostly figure in the story she had carefully crafted, and Julian's distance made her feel uneasy about her place in the story's unfolding.

Mila stood by the door, her body tense but her face blank. The publisher's office had sharp angles that made her feel trapped, but she moved through it with quiet grace, as if the piles of papers and quiet whispers were a world she didn't belong to. Voices rose and fell around her, and accusations were thinly veiled behind polite tones. But Mila kept her voice steady, with her lips pressed together in a line that hid the storm behind her eyes. She felt guilty, like the smell of old coffee in the air, but she met the weight of suspicion with an outward calm that gave nothing away. At this moment, she wasn't part of the chaos; she was just watching a story she wanted to rewrite in her head slowly fall apart.

She looked at the publisher, a man whose every look seemed to be full of questions he wouldn't say out loud. The flicker of the fluorescent light made shadows under his tired eyes, making him look older than he was. She realised she was pulling away, separating her thoughts from the events that had brought her here, and refusing to join in on the story that others were putting together so quickly. The editorial room, with its sterile walls and broken conversations, was a place where truth was a valuable thing that was difficult to come by for people with weak egos. Mila could feel the pressure building just below the surface, like a current she could sense but not touch. It was as if her presence was a quiet ripple in a storm that was already going on.

Even though she didn't say anything, Mila's mind was racing with bits and pieces of the night before: sharp words exchanged in tense hallways, an unexpected shove, and the door slamming that echoed too loudly in her chest. She thought back to when Julian had tripped and the look in his eyes that changed from anger to something she couldn't read. Fear had made her run away, and the thick taste of panic that coated her throat made her feel empty inside, where doubt had rooted deep in her bones. But now, standing in this room where every whispered accusation could become an anchor, she told herself that she hadn't touched the last thread that was coming apart. She wasn't a murderer or a conspirator; she was just a woman stuck between a story she didn't recognise anymore and the need to hold on to parts of herself that were still whole.

The short conversation with the publisher was full of tension. His handshake was firm but not too firm, and his voice was calm but had a hint of suspicion that Mila could hear. She could smell the faint smell of cigars mixed with the bitter smell of cold, black coffee that had been left on the desk for a long time. These little things brought her back to a moment that felt both unreal and very real. There was a lot of tension in the office, like a fog that made it difficult to think and made every breath feel like work. She chose her words carefully when she answered his questions. Each one carried the weight of her silence about the truth. But she kept her eyes on the worn leather chair across from her, the only place she could picture herself slipping away from it all.

Mila pulled away from the events that had led to Julian's death as the publisher asked her questions. She remembered the last manuscript she had taken, which was hidden deep in her bag and too dangerous to show but too important to throw away. The shadows in the room turned into shapes she knew were masks—people who were good at hiding their secrets and reputations. She watched as their stories unfolded like threads on an old loom, each trying to make a version of Julian's end that worked for them. But Mila wasn't part of their plan. Her story was different; it was full of fear and lies, but she didn't have to take the blame they wanted to give her. The fight that ended in a knot, the stolen manuscript, and the escape fuelled by fear: it wasn't a plan to kill; it was a desperate attempt to stay alive in a story she never wanted to be a part of.

Mila's silence became her shield in a room where everyone wanted to be in charge. She knew what was going on: the slow tightening of a noose made of lies and assumptions. But she didn't say anything because she knew that saying something would mean admitting to a reality that was too complicated for the neat stories other people wanted. Mila saw the publisher's eyes flicker with doubt and calculation. She realised that sometimes the strongest thing to say was nothing at all. It was a quiet refusal to get involved in a story that could never fully explain what had really happened. At this weak point, her distance wasn't indifference; it was a survival instinct, a way to protect the fragile threads of truth she carried alone.

When silence is so strong that it feels like a person is there, it changes everything that comes after. Mila was able to step back from the accusing looks and heavy air because she was able to control herself during those short conversations. One useful truth becomes clear: when memories and motives are at odds, the best thing to do is to stay on the sidelines and watch. You can keep a story alive and even rewrite it later, with the clarity and control that only distance can give, by watching, listening, and carefully choosing when to speak and when to be quiet.

Detective Byrne had always thought that knowing how her suspects' money worked could help her solve the case. Byrne knew she had to dig deep when Sloane Porter came onto her radar. Sloane was a very private person, but Byrne thought it was worth figuring out what was going on with her money. As soon as she asked for bank statements, credit reports, and tax returns, she began to put together a story of growing losses and dead ends. It was clear that Sloane was not the successful agent she seemed to be; her money was in trouble, and she had many overdue bills.

As Byrne looked over the papers, things started to make more sense. Sloane was personally involved in Julian Vane's failed legacy, which left her with debts she couldn't pay back. The publishing deal that once promised her fame now felt like a chain tightening around her ankle. She had taken out loans to pay for

Julian's last project, and the publishers were demanding their money right away. Byrne saw a pattern: late payments, cheques that had not been cashed, and a string of unpaid bills that showed someone was about to go broke.

Sloane's credit report showed a perfect storm of problems: high credit use, maxed-out credit cards, and a lot of bounced cheques. Byrne's gut told her that Sloane's actions before and after Julian's death could be explained by her desperation. She was worried about more than just losing her reputation; she was worried about losing everything she had left. The feeling that Sloane was about to go broke gave him a quiet but strong reason to act. Byrne thought that this push towards despair might have made Sloane do something rash or, worse, plan things out so that she could protect herself from the empire that was falling apart around her.

Byrne figured out that Sloane was responsible for Julian's unpaid debts after doing some careful research. It was also easy to see why her motives might change because she was in a bad financial situation. It wasn't just because they felt sorry for Julian's fading fame; it was also about protecting themselves. Sloane believed that by portraying Julian's life as a tragic tale of failure and decline, she could conceal her own collapse. It made sense to Byrne that she would want to change the story of Julian's death to save her reputation and avoid the crushing weight of bankruptcy.

Byrne also had to figure out how Sloane hid her money problems to find out these things. Byrne understood that people often conceal their most embarrassing truths, such as shredded receipts, hidden accounts, or unreported money. Sloane's silence about money was very loud. Byrne thought she was hiding more than she was showing—maybe even making up papers or hiding money. Byrne knew that the stakes were so high for Sloane that this could change how she played her next move. Byrne's job was to find out if a woman who was about to lose everything would make disastrous decisions, like planning a death that fit a perfect story.

Byrne finally realised that Sloane's financial problems were more than just a minor detail; they were the key to solving the whole mystery. Knowing someone's debts, how desperate they are, and why they want to change the story can change the investigation's focus completely. When it comes to motives based on financial ruin, it's often the small, hidden choices made when you're weak that bridge the gap between doubt and truth. Byrne made a mental note: Don't ever ignore the power of financial details; they often reveal the truth behind the calm facade.

Chapter Ten

THE STOLEN MANUSCRIPT

(11:00 AM)

Mary stood there for a while, her heart beating like a train that had gone off the tracks. Julian's office was a mess, and she couldn't concentrate straight since she had too much on her mind. She took a deep breath and scented the old paper and stale coffee. The scent made her think of the late nights and early mornings they had spent together. No amount of writing or notes could mask the fear that was eating away at her, making her hands shake as she pushed them aside.

She started to furiously go through piles of papers that weren't even stacked correctly. Each piece of paper had recollections of their past conversations, which were now simply whispers in the stale air. Julian was a genius, but he made things very hard to understand. Mary wanted to know how things got to this point. "Julian, have you seen my notes?" she questioned, her voice scarcely audible and cracking with terror. She wanted him to answer, but she was stuck in this maze of his obsession.

The dim light made shadows creep down the walls, which made the room feel like it was getting smaller.

Mary could hardly see anything clearly, and the gloom felt like it was closing in on her. There were mysteries and unanswered questions in every corner of the room. She was breathing quickly and shallowly, and the quiet around her made her nervous. Every time she heard paper rustling, it sounded bad to her. She remembered the last time she saw Julian, a picture of withering brilliance, engrossed in his words while she stood on the sidelines. The recollections made her panic worse and made the knot in her stomach even tighter.

She thought that every book she read was about their life together, and every personal notebook she glanced at was full of his thoughts, which were sometimes brilliant and sometimes bizarre. She felt terrible as she pushed the journal away. Was she losing herself in this search while he lay there, possibly dead? But she couldn't help it. She had to find her notes since they were the last thing she had to connect with him and the last chance she had. The chaotic piles appeared to make fun of her, reminding her of how hard it had been for them to converse with each other and how far away they had gone.

Sloane sat calmly in her office, where the warm light from a desk lamp produced long shadows on the walls that were covered in framed contracts and old images of her prior accomplishments. The room smelt a little like old paper and stale coffee, which she associated with long hours and short deadlines. Detective Byrne asked Sloane about the lost manuscript, and her face kept calm. It was a controlled mask that disguised the shock that was running through her body. Her eyes were still, but her mind was racing. She went over every moment and every interaction, looking for the thread that she might have missed or not spotted. Things were going crazy around her, but she stayed calm because she knew how hazardous it was to display doubt, especially now.

That day kept coming back to her mind. When she heard that Julian had died, it was so unexpected and painful that it stayed with her like a vague ache. She remembered stepping into his flat, where it was hushed and there was a slight smell of tobacco and something else she couldn't place. She didn't notice anything unusual until she arrived at his writing desk. That's when the missing manuscript hit her like a dagger. It felt like a mistake, a massive blunder in a situation that was already too unstable to deal with. Sloane's gut told her to be calm and seem like the agent who knew what was going on, even though she didn't. Denying any knowledge was her only way to avoid suspicion and blame, which she had to do to keep her job and her weak grip on the truth.

She remembered the slight uneasiness that came over her when she chatted to acquaintances, police officers, and the occasional journalist with hungry eyes who came to see her. She felt like she was being jabbed with needles every time someone asked her a question about the book, but she was cautious not to let anyone see that she was angry. She had never been part of the secret of the missing pages, and she was unable to explain or justify their absence. When she thought about saying she didn't know, she felt like she was betraying Julian's legacy, herself, and everything she had worked for. Sloane knew that if she made a mistake, people would quickly blame her, so she nodded pleasantly, provided scripted answers, and kept the discussion going without letting on that she didn't know everything.

The stolen manuscript was more than simply an item; it was the key to finding out or making Julian's meticulously prepared plot even better. Sloane's money difficulties were like a shadow over her, making the stakes even higher. She had seen publishers grow mad and ask for more, and each delay was making her account balance less. The scandal and the loss of Julian's last effort, which she had hoped would save them both, were unnecessary for her. She didn't steal anything, even though she was under a lot of stress. She had to accept that it was out of her hands, even though it fouled up all of her plans.

Sloane kept saying no to everything, not because she was lying, but because it was the only way to stay alive. She realised that authority in the literary world was a fragile thing and that saying she didn't know something or was weak may give others the upper hand. There was no room for weakness. There was a lot going on in her head behind the calm surface. She was putting together pieces of recollection and scanning through the timeline for hints that could take her to a place she hadn't been brave enough to go yet. The stolen manuscript was like a ghost in the room, always there and always threatening to tell her things she wasn't ready to hear. She kept playing her role, calm and steady, hoping that the answers would come out without pulling her into the tempest she was most terrified of.

Keep in mind that when you're stressed, looking calm doesn't always mean you're okay. Sometimes, silence or denial might be a sign of fear, perplexity, or even simple ignorance. It's just as important to pay attention to what people don't say as it is to pay attention to what they do say.

Mila sat alone in her little, dark apartment and looked

at the jumbled manuscript on her desk. The yellowed pages had been handled so much that their edges were slightly bent. The weak light from a desk lamp cast lengthy shadows on them. She was scared and excited at the same time, and her fingers shook as she carefully traced the scrawled lines. The scent of old paper and ink brought her back to the present as she got set to read Julian's sad confession. The words on the pages seemed to be whispering secrets that only she could hear, truths that could change her life forever.

Julian Vane kept the text a secret until he died. It was a hidden gem. The papers featured his unedited, honest thoughts—things he never wanted anyone else to see. Mila stretched the papers out in front of her and saw she was holding more than just a confession. She had her future, her job, and maybe even her freedom in her hands. She had worked hard and fought for a long time to come to this point, to locate the key to Julian's last act. She got ready to read the words that may make her famous or ruin her life. Her hands shook and her heart raced. Every time the pages crackled, it felt like the weight of what she was about to learn grew heavier.

Her eyes went quickly across the scrawled lines, carefully reading each word. The writing was jagged and emotional, and sometimes it was all over the place, and other times it was frighteningly accurate. Julian's tone was honest; he showed times when he was weak, furious, and seeking to control other people. Mila thought that these pages held the truth of his death, the portions that no one else could figure out or even suspect. This was her proof that Julian's last act wasn't just a random event or a tragedy; it was a perfectly prepared performance. The manuscript also exposed Julian's darker side: his desire to leave behind a legacy of lies, secrets, and blood. She knew that the way she used each word could make it a weapon or a shield.

As Mila carefully turned the pages, her mind raced with ideas. The papers hinted at secrets Julian had held from everyone, even her, and reasons that went deep. She pondered about how her revelation would hurt her job with every word she wrote. She thought about the interviews, the headlines, and the literary awards—the recognition she desired but was too scared to ask for. But there was a worse sensation underneath her goals:

remorse. She could still see the fight when Julian pushed her and she collapsed. She wondered if her panic had changed from fear to remorse and if she was too responsible for his injuries. She knew as she read on that Julian had known about this weak area in his life all along and had used it to obtain what he wanted by telling a story that only he could control.

As she read on, Mila recognised that the book that had been taken from her could be her strongest bargaining tool. The things it says could be made into a captivating story that would grab the attention of readers, critics, and publishers. She might explain that her relationship with Julian was more than simply an affair; it was a deal, a secret that had to do with his innermost fears and desires. While she spoke at podiums or was interviewed about her work, Julian's revelation hung over her like a shadow. The text was what made her keep going. The manuscript showed that she could reach her full potential and make a name for herself in the literary world, but it also had the power to wreck everything if she let the truth slip away. As she read the horrible confessions that Julian had penned himself, she thought she had the power.

The faint sound of the overhead light and the clean smell of the interrogation room blended together. Detective Byrne walked in with a cool demeanour, but her instincts were on high alert. She had seen a lot of people at this table, but tonight Mila Novak's face struck out to her as unusually scary. Mila was slumped over in her chair, and her hands were moving swiftly in her lap, which revealed how agitated she was. She gave off a mix of fear and resolve that made the room feel smaller.

When Byrne sat down across from her, the mood changed. The investigator leaned forward, her eyes piercing but calm, as she got ready to talk about what transpired that night. Mila's heart beat as she thought about every little thing that happened during the battle with Julian, how he had looked at her in that last minute, and the horrible feeling that followed. She knew that the questioning would come soon and fiercely, and she got ready for the inevitable digging into her alibi.

Mila took a long breath to settle her voice before she began to relate her side of the incident. Her remarks came out smoothly, as if she had rehearsed them in her head. She said:

"I got to Julian's house around six," trying to seem cool. "We ate dinner. It was a normal night." But the small shake in her voice gave her away. She remembered how tense things had been that night, and her heart raced.

Byrne nodded and kept a tight eye out for any signs of truth or deception.

"What did you fight about?" she enquired, putting a pen over a pad of paper.

There was a lot of weight in the question. Mila paused for a bit and looked down at her hands, which were shaking.

"Just some things going wrong in my life. Not a big deal."

She hoped the investigator couldn't see through the

holes in her mask. But as Mila talked, her carefully thought-out replies started to trip over each other, and she showed indicators of guilt, including a twitch in her eye, a shortness of breath, and a slightly raised brow.

Byrne kept an eye on her every move, knowing that there were stories beneath Mila's placid answers. Everything seemed like every "I don't remember" and "it was all fine" was more of a fight than a confession. The two women became friends, and a war of wits broke out in the little space. Byrne, who was skilled at reading people's feelings, could tell that Mila was having a difficult time even though she was attempting to be calm in the storm she had produced.

CHAPTER ELEVEN

THE WIFE'S "ALIBI"

(12:30 PM)

Mary pushed the door to the café open. The quiet hum of the hospital's small café hit her like a wave that was both familiar and unwelcome. The strong smell of brewed coffee mixed with the sound of cups clinking together and people talking softly. She looked around the room until she saw her cardiology coworker Beth already sitting in the corner by the window. The sunlight pooled around her, making a soft glow that stood out from the tension that was building up inside Mary. Mary sat down and folded her hands neatly, hiding the anxiety that had been eating away at her all morning.

Beth smiled tiredly and said: "You look like you needed this more than I do."

She pushed a mug of black coffee towards Mary. Their lunches had become a ritual, a rare chance to relax in the fast-paced hospital. Mary nodded and looked quickly at the empty chair across from her. It was Julian's absence that was weighing on her the most.

"He isn't doing well," she said softly, her voice barely

above the soft buzz of the café. "He's getting worse, but it's like he's backing off before the worst happens."

Beth reached out, which was nice, but Mary pulled back a little.

"You don't understand," she said, her voice calmer now. "It's not just his health. He's... going away in ways I can't get to. The man I married — the writer I loved — feels like a ghost trapped inside his own body."

There was no accusation, just a tired frustration. Julian's health had been getting worse slowly, but Mary felt the weight of it all the time. She tried everything, from appointments to treatments to interventions, but nothing seemed to work.

As the conversation went on, Mary said things she usually kept to herself because of her job.

"He wasn't always like this," she said, looking at the chipped edge of her coffee cup. "It's like he's trying to hurt himself on purpose by refusing help and pushing people away. And the worst part? He's doing it just to spite me."

Her voice dropped, and the bitterness in it surprised her. Julian had always been proud of her work, but now his anger was coming out in their conversations, sharp and corrosive.

"You get mad at him?" Beth asked carefully, sensing the thin line Mary was walking between love and anger.

Mary thought for a moment before saying: "Yeah, sometimes. It's tiring to act like everything is fine when it's not. I feel like I'm losing him all over again when he lashes out or goes quiet."

The noise of the café faded into the background as Mary let herself say what she'd been keeping to herself: Julian's illness wasn't just physical; it was breaking up the life they'd built together.

Mary's words hung in the air, and unspoken questions ran through them: was Julian's decline a surrender or a secret rebellion? Was she just a caretaker now, or was she something else? These doubts weighed her down, making the afternoon sun feel colder than it should have.

Beth moved in her seat because she felt like the conversation needed to go somewhere more real.

"Where were you yesterday afternoon?"

"Why?" she asked, not because she was suspicious but because she was genuinely curious.

Mary looked her straight in the eye.

"At the hospital," she said simply, her voice steady even though the tension was still there. "I had a scheduled cardiac consult, and then I had to do paperwork that kept me at my desk until almost seven."

Mary needed to stress the routine detail—a structured, documented timeline that resisted the chaos surrounding Julian's situation.

She went on to talk about the ups and downs of her day in clear detail: early morning rounds, a complicated patient who needed all of her attention, and a quick lunch she grabbed between meetings. The sterile smell of antiseptic, the beeping of monitors, and the bright lights in the hospital all set the stage for a day that didn't allow for any side trips or secrets.

Mary added: "Of course there are logs, time-stamped

records, sign-ins, the usual."

It was a boring kind of proof, but it made her story feel real in a way that was almost too normal compared to everything else.

For Mary, this excuse was both a way to protect herself and a way to admit what she had done. It kept people from being suspicious of her, but it also made her feel alone. She was at work and not with Julian, so she couldn't stop him from falling apart. And even though she didn't want to know it, it was a truth that she couldn't escape. The hospital schedules, the patient notes, and the steady rhythm of clinical life all came together to make her presence unquestionable, even when her heart was torn between doubt and guilt.

Sloane was crouched over her laptop, and her fingers moved rapidly and deftly across the keys. The room was dark, and the only light came from the flashing financial charts on the screen. She was very concentrated as she went over Julian's investment portfolio and didn't miss a thing. She realised what was at risk, and time was running short. She had to move swiftly to get Julian the big advance he needed for his new book. Stocks have to be sold right away to earn cash before the publisher's deadline. She had to decide what to sell to earn the most money with the least loss. Every second counted. It was a precise balancing act that needed calm precision even while tension levels were mounting.

It was evident that she was nervous behind her eyes. She realised that telling people she was going to sell some of her stuff might raise their eyebrows, but she couldn't wait. She was in this condition since Julian's sales didn't go through and her debt kept mounting. Selling her stocks would provide her cash, but it would also mean losing money on investments she had once believed in. She thought about the dates when the books would come out, how the publishers wanted their money back, and how her reputation was on the line. She rapidly clicked through the pages and chose the shares that were most likely to sell quickly and not cause too much trouble in the long run. Every sale was like tearing a small hole in the finely woven picture she had built for herself, but it had to be done to avert disaster.

She moved with purpose, her thoughts balancing the two realities of requiring money and the heavy load of her own private intentions. She felt a little better and a little nervous as she saw the numbers alter as the orders came in. She sold equities to pay back the loan Julian had got, which was a modest fix for a big problem. This process provided her more time, but it also established a labyrinth of deceit. The city outside was tranquil, not knowing that a hurricane was going on under her fingers. The chamber smelt faintly of paper and cold metal, which made her think of the world she lived in, where things could be purchased, sold, and wiped in an instant.

Sloane sat down in the leather chair opposite from the table. She was still worried about how quickly she had to sell Julian's stocks. She filled a glass with chilled white wine and took a slow sip. The light sparkled off the cool surface of the wine. She groped for a little oyster while she sat there in the solitude. The salty taste on her tongue felt strangely right, as if the brine reminded her of the short, sharp decisions she had just made. The thin shell in her fingers reminded her of how rapidly life and fortunes can change, just like the creature inside. Her thoughts kept going over the details as she ate. She wasn't sure if the money she had just obtained would be enough or if she would have to do something more dramatic.

The oysters' salty taste and the wine's smoothness made her feel peaceful for a moment, which let her forget about how anxious she was getting. She stared out the window at the blinking city lights below and wondered if her hasty money-making would last until the final minute or if the weight of her concealed motives would make it all fall apart. She thought of how hard it was to keep up the frail front she put on for everyone else, Julian's secret intention to kill her, and her own financial collapse. The cold wine and raw oysters were like a shield that helped her feel better right away in the middle of her confused thoughts. She knew she had to keep up the act and make sure everything went well, or the truth may come out and everything could fall apart.

Mila had just gone into a cosy cafe; her eyes needed to adjust to the dim light in a wonderful contrast to the street right outside. Entering the moment, the strong scent of roasted coffee beans mixed with the sweetness of fresh bakery wrapped around her, embracing her warmly. She took a deep breath to hide the fluttering in her heart. Dressed all in black, she had an air of casual professionalism about her that seemed suitable for discussing her latest manuscript with Sloane, her agent. The café was clogged with the low murmur of other patrons and the chinking of cups, but Mila's focus was still on the job ahead while her heart raced with fear and excitement.

Sloane arrived shortly after, her presence still commanding in the relaxed atmosphere of the cafe. Settling down at a small corner table, they were brought two steaming cups of tea and took scones lying halfway eaten on top of a plate between them. They exchanged compliments, Mila's mind working furiously. She asked Sloane some leading questions about their mutual goals, a little mystified look on her face. Sloane, who was normally reasonable and reserved, appeared unusually lively today; her eyes gleamed unreadable things. Mila sensed an electric feeling in the air, like the café itself was holding its breath for them to talk.

In an uncertain tone Mila brought up an 'award-winning' idea that had sprung up in her mind. Her voice was almost a whisper, laced with both excitement and caution. It was not just any solicitation but an opportunity which could change her career forever, as she had long dreamed about. Would Sloane realise its potential? Would she see in Mila herself the dangerous edge of ambition? As she discussed her concept, the very air seemed to thicken, her eyes glued to Sloane's face for every suggestion of encouragement or hint at hesitation. Sloane leaned back, fingers steepled, carefully pondering Mila's proposal. At that exact moment the cafe background fell away, leaving them just two people inside a tight sphere of strained ambition and unfulfilled dreams, both acutely conscious about the stakes.

Detective Byrne sat back in the hard chair in the interrogation room and looked at the grainy security footage on the monitor again. The clock on the wall ticked steadily, which was very different from the way her stomach felt. Mary West's movements were clear: calm, precise, and almost like she was rehearsing. The times matched up perfectly from the time Mary left the hospital to the time Julian Vane died. The surveillance camera caught her going to the store, stopping for a short time at a coffee shop, and then getting home twenty minutes before Julian's last recorded moments. Every frame and every beep on the timestamp matched what she said.

The forensic reports showed that Mary was not at the scene of the crime at the time of death. Her timeline was backed up by medical records and hospital swipe cards. The alibi was so strong that it made Byrne uneasy. It seemed almost too perfect, like someone had practiced the movements to fit a story instead of the truth.

Even though the evidence was clear, Byrne's instincts made her uneasy. Mary's testimony sounded too polished. That day, the room was eerily quiet. No one moved or made mistakes in their speech; only the soft tap of a pen and Mary's steady breathing could be heard. It was the kind of calmness you expect from a professional, but it was almost robotic. Byrne knew that the people who were the quietest were sometimes the ones who had the biggest secrets. Mary's movements were so precise and her memories were so clear that they made me suspicious: could this alibi have been made with knowledge of every camera angle and every witness? She had learnt that perfect alibis often meant that something was being kept secret just below the surface. The question wasn't if Mary was there or not. It was a matter of whether she was telling the truth or a well-written lie meant to cover up something much worse.

Byrne pulled out the forensic reports again and looked over the edges, making notes about small details about the physical evidence and chemical residues. There was nothing at the scene that pointed to Mary. There were no fingerprints out of place, no signs of her perfume or sweat, and no signs of forced entry or struggle. The reports were very detailed. But there was a shadow of doubt that Byrne couldn't ignore in the silence that followed these reports. She thought she was looking at a puzzle where one of the biggest pieces had been smoothed out on purpose to hide its real edges. This alibi looked good on paper, but it seemed like it had been polished so much that it lost its natural rough-ness. Byrne kept thinking about the video over and over again: how Mary rested her hands on the grocery cart and how she moved slowly and easily from scene to scene. It was too strict. Like a show, almost.

Byrne started to notice small differences, like whispers that were barely audible under the loud facts. There is a small difference between the time Mary said she called Julian and the call records. A thirty-second gap in the security footage that no one had noticed before. The evidence technicians found a floral and sharp smell that hung around the edge of an empty bottle in the kitchen. Cleaning agent. The smell of sterility made it seem like Mary had been cleaning not long after the time of death. Byrne thought about the clean shine of a polished counter, the sound of bleach on a cloth, and the unspoken need to get rid of everything that a camera couldn't see. These little things slowly crept into her mind, making her think of a calm surface that was barely hiding a lot of trouble underneath.

The more Byrne thought about how calm Mary looked, the more it looked like it was planned. Mary's memories of each moment were too smooth, like the kind of clarity that comes from practicing a story over and over again in a quiet room. Byrne wondered if even the best alibi could really hide the truth. What if the heart that was shaking with guilt or fear was still beating wildly under that calm exterior? Byrne felt the weight of each question that had not been answered pressing against her ribs. Mary's story was well organised and didn't make her feel bad, but Byrne's gut disagreed. Truth wasn't always neat; it wasn't a perfect script delivered without a hitch. The sterile cleanliness, the precise timeline, and the lingering smell of disinfectant all told me that this story was too perfect. Byrne chose to look deeper, not just at the evidence but also at the spaces between them and what Mary's calm face didn't say.

It's easy to trust the surface in situations like this. But Byrne knew that when things seemed too easy, it was usually a sign to pay more attention, listen more closely, and trust the feeling of unease over the polished story. The lesson: when checking alibis, look for the strange things that don't seem to fit, like a strange smell, a split second that isn't accounted for, or a calm that doesn't seem to break. These small hints can say more than the clearest testimony ever could.

CHAPTER TWELVE

THE SEARCH HISTORY

(1:30 PM)

Mary sat in her softly lit office all by herself; the glow of her laptop cast upon her land a faint blue shine. She kept her eyes on the search bar, trembling as she typed in medical terms that looked like alphabet soup. Every key struck seemed to weigh heavier than before, her heart racing between doubt and justification. The room was thick with silence; the one noise breaking it was the soft clicking of keys and also her whispering breaths. She knew what she was looking for, but the weight of her own actions made her stomach squeal with anger.

She was in search of precise dosage figures for drugs and, more particularly, information on just how many of Julian's tablets could cause harm. Checking was a case not of curiosity but rather fear: fear that he might slip away, fear something might befall him over which she had no control at all. Her heart beat softly in her chest as she switched over details; images began to blossom in her mind of how many pills could be fatal, but not so many that it would reveal her intentions immediately: poisoning him outright wasn't the main concern – it was about learning enough through practice. She could head off any potential disaster, be it by misadventure or deliberately.

As she thought up a response, her fingers hung over the keys. She had said ad nauseam that it was just research. Before she could argue with herself. It helped her think of the worst that could happen so as to prevent such disasters, all the while she was trying to console him. That to herself one way after another, so she could convince the subconscious that she was trying only to prevent a disaster and not actually arranging one. But it was hidden under the surface, this truth, not as simple as a worry. In some recess of her mind, a voice told her she was trying to get ready—just in case.

What was clear was that she needed to change and saw no other source at this moment than her laptop for looking. At that time, she read carefully composed articles, followed medical guidelines word for word, and turned over forums where doctors and patients discussed drug dosage. The information was precise, almost clinical in nature, and detailed safe ranges to dangerous thresholds. Snippets were copied and pasted from sources into her private document, and she took care as she surfed the web to cover up tracks. Her eyes tediously read all those details over again and yet again, trying to absorb every mixture of variables. It occurred to her that if necessary she would employ this knowledge not for hurt but prevention — so when those chaotic, uncertain hours came, at least there would be no mishaps. Still, there was a sneaking suspicion that with her knowledge of such details, she would also feel more confident in a situation as unpredictable as this, even if to gain control might mean crossing some invisible border.

The world around her office was blissfully unaware of the secret searches she was taking time away from work to conduct. Drawing of a hand on the wall, the sound of spring in the city leaked through the shut window, a dampened but insistent reminder that life went on. Julian had often joked about the unpredictability of life and death; he would pooh-pooh people's worries with a shrug.

Fuelled by her own fears, she was asking questions behind closed doors. Staring at the screen, hoping no one would think her search was anything less remarkable, she wondered if anyone would understand that a woman really concerned for the health of her husband sought only information and truth to cure him. There was one thought in her heart: she was frightened—fear prodding her to do things she otherwise wouldn't. Her small private office was both sanctuary and jail, holding the secret that she prayed would never come out. As she closed the browser window, her hands were still slightly sticky. She tells herself she was to keep it quiet, cover the speed traps with a calm front. Even if her motivations seemed reasonable, the fears were deeply ingrained in her psyche. To others, the brief research might be trivial or even seem innocent, but it was a last resort for her – a means of protection against what came tomorrow. Tomorrow the whole world would change again, and right now she had to keep her secrets close to her heart so that no one else knew about them: in the dark corners of a frightened and terrified mind. Nevertheless, every time she saw Julian's bottle of medication on the shelf, the knowledge of what she had searched for stalked silently, heavily in her thoughts.

Sloane Porter directed all her attention to the work before her, the day full of business. She also constantly kept in mind the various problems connected with Julian Vane's career and the confidence which lay in his reputation. Before long, she had meticulously arranged what plans she could make to follow after he died, but nothing warned her that the truth lay just beneath the surface of everyday life.

While she was shuffling papers and answering phone calls, Julian's computer was quietly building a different edifice with its history of searches. The story painted was far removed from how things looked depending on who was examining them. Every mouse click or keystroke made revealed secrets Sloane could not see. She flipped idly through drafts of Julian's final manuscript, and her mind danced with ideas about the financial implications of his death. Would her agency survive this loss, or was it time to spin this tragedy into a marketable story?

Despite bearing the weight of despair, Julian's death felt like an opportunity. His computer's search history was quietly hinting at manipulation. It detailed the trips that Sloane ignored while attempting to present loss as a compelling story of genius. The more Sloane sought to protect her interests and Julian's legacy, the deeper she entrenched herself in self-denial. The whispers of the search histories told of Julian's detailed planning. From that digital abyss came reams of comparative material about the day he died and the way he sought to control his story until revealing intentions she never dreamed possible. Unbeknownst to her, this coded language of secrets was pointing to something very dark indeed – a signal that she missed amidst all this ballyhoo over a flawless narrative. The concealed details of Julian's online behaviour could strip away some of the mystery of his actions. It appeared that he had been working to a schedule, meticulously setting up an opera that would ensnare his family.

Sloane's lack of curiosity meant that she missed these signals entirely. The revelations hidden in his history of searches, unfiltered and raw, held a wealth of insights into a life collapsing while she prepped her version of the tragedy. Julian's plans, menacing and complicated, hung silent in those forgotten clicks, revealing a truth that would remain with the women he controlled forever. Her thoughts extended only as far as what she deemed important, a legacy clouded by personal mistakes and financial ruin. Sloane did not see that she was positioning herself among the refuse piled up by Julian's decisions. Her ambitions veiled his truths, creating a dissonance that marked his final moments. Had she stopped to listen and decode the sense of urgency hidden in those daily Internet searches – which seemed so simple and straightforward – perhaps she might have reconciled many misconceptions about Julian and herself.

Mila leaned on the worn fabric and absent fingers. She was right on the edge of the couch, and she could hardly force herself not to think of what lay ahead this evening. Outlines of the night fell into being through a low hum from the city, drifting through the half-open window and mixing with remains of rain in air gone stale. Her phone lay face down upon the coffee table with a muted buzz, its only link to life. And yet in her mind there was no peace. She kept replaying that argument with Julian, the sharp snap of his voice, and the sudden weight as he fell. There was guilt there too, but she savagely pushed it back behind layer upon layer of training and self-protection.

Tonight, Mila told herself she would be calm and collected, the way she always had to be. On the surface for Mila this evening was simple in two parts: close friends, wine and laughter to hide the knot of bitterness coiling in her stomach. As she hadn't checked messages for hours and had seen none of the news, it was easier not to. Nor, easier still, was there to weigh down her consciousness any reflection on the dark manuscript squeezed inside her bag – that one last secret she had taken. Although her phone search history was there, locked behind a password Mila herself barely remembered, she was unaware of what anyone else might find if they looked.

She was focused simply on the noise she could control, the illusion of normalcy that she strove to maintain. Her browsing that day had been casual and without great meaning. She scrolled through art pages, bookmarked recipes she would never cook, and glanced at reviews for a documentary on writers who disappeared from public view. Nothing had high stakes; none of it showed the storm brewing inside her. But however benign her mouse clicks and searches might seem, a kind of restless energy swirled underneath. Mila was not only combing through options and regrets; she was also trying to put right the jumbled memories left by fright and shadow. In her thoughts, things seemed manageable, but rising within her was a suppressed chaos that was still unchart-ed even by those around her.

Detective Byrne sat at her computer, her eyes narrowing as she scrolled through Mary Toege's online activities. The screen was filled with search queries that appeared perfectly legitimate at first glance, but a pattern quickly emerged. Amidst the usual medical reports and cooking tips, one search caught her eye: 'How much of a certain drug is virtually certain to be fatal? '

That phrase was coldly deliberate. Byrne's experience told her that this was not a question asked casually. It hinted that someone was trying to find a way to take a life without anyone knowing, without any suspicion being aroused. That search alone made the idea of premeditation inevitable in her mind. It wasn't just careless planning: it was purposeful, with the clear intention to kill. Byrne knew this was a lead of major significance and needed to be thoroughly checked out.

The in-depth exploration of the search history brought even more chilling details to light. Mary studied specific doses and how they affected the heart, read up on items about overdose symptoms and drug contradictions, and even explored the weakest point – how much of a drug would make death quick but not disorderly, quietly enough that people didn't know what was going on. In her game searches, she typed phrases like 'heart medication overdose', 'fast-acting lethal dose', and 'symptoms of heart poisoning'. These searches were not arbitrary. They were designed, precise, and intent upon accumulating the hows and whys of killing silently. It suggested someone who was not only frightened or confused but was actively contemplating and planning to end Julian's life. Byrne's instincts told her that behind Mary's friendly mask of calm lay a darker, hidden motive.

Even more disturbing was the fact that Mary's web searches were running parallel with the days leading up to Julian's death. She was extraordinarily thorough about Julian's dosage, for example, all but dictating doses almost obsessively and always by his side while he took his pills.

Mary's search history was painting quite a picture for Byrne. Somehow. At some point in the future—whether it was designed of intention or accidental, Byrnes did not even want to conjecture—Mary would in all likelihood be giving these pills to Julian. Under such circumstances, what on earth would a wife want with this kind of information? Keith couldn't believe it; it seemed to him (if ever something difficult to pin down made sense in the light of day) Mary was using these web searches as a job interview for getting rid of Julian. Yet the further she probed, the more obvious it became:

Mary was not simply concerned for Julian's health but actively pursuing an escape route for which she regarded herself as infallible. It all made her a prime suspect, and Byrne knew the next thing she would find could well determine whether that suspicion was confirmed or shattered apart. When Byrne assembled the jigsaw puzzle, each thread of information came into focus. The search history was a guide, leading directly to long-term planning.

The contemplative bit wasn't out and simply a slip of mind or idle curiosity; it was an act undertaken in preparation. With her police officer's sense honed, Byrne realised that this matter wasn't just about which unit had the most compelling motive but also, more fundamentally, about understanding intentions behind quiet movements. She also thought about the kind of person Mary was – calm, rational, with an apparent detachment. Such a personality was often capable of careful scheming, its malice hidden behind a serene facade. Byrne thought about the weight of earlier instances, when normal-looking people buried amazing secrets, and she wondered whether it was a crucial piece of hidden truth she needed to reveal as she continued with her investigation tomorrow or if it would prove to be nothing more than a diversion.

Chapter Thirteen

THE THREAT

(2:00 PM)

Mary West stood at her kitchen counter, where the morning sun came in through the window and made patterns on the tile floor. The smell of freshly brewed coffee filled the air, warm and inviting. But she felt a heaviness in her chest that the aroma couldn't lift. As a cardiologist, she was used to the realities of life and death, yet nothing could prepare her for the mess she was now entangled in. Julian, her husband, had always been a complicated person, but his recent decline had taken away the respect she had for him. It gleamed from him once, but now it felt tarnished, worn out. Half of her wanted to nurse him through his suffering, while the other half boiled with resentment and shame for his weakness.

Her day began not with a supportive husband, but with this weight of uncertainty. Did he care what condition he was in? The rash of self-neglect haunted her thoughts. She stirred her coffee without noticing the steam that was swirling around it. This was a sign that their relationship was getting colder.

As she flicked through her phone, messages from friends

asking how Julian was feeling felt almost mocking. They couldn't comprehend the grasp of helplessness she felt. To them, he was still a celebrated author, a genius who could easily navigate through any storm, while he was losing himself inside the walls of their home. The awards that used to hang on their walls now felt like heavy chains around her neck.

Mary had faced many challenges in her career, commanding respect in a male-dominated field. Yet the chaos Julian had brought into her life was unfamiliar. She stood among the shiny medical journals and books full of the latest research and felt how different her work life was from her personal life. She put her perfectly manicured fingers on the counter and tried to keep her stomach from tightening. Each day brought increasing anxiety, and every action she took was clouded by suspicion—was he genuinely ill, or was this merely a dramatic ploy to elicit pity? He had stubbornly refused to accept her insistence that he needed help. The more she urged, the more he retreated.

Self-doubt gnawed at her thoughts. During her long, exhausting hours at the hospital, she parked her emotions deep down, while during quick glances at home, she tried to placate the mounting tension. Was she unnaturally calm about things that should have made her angry? She was calm and sure at work, but at home, she was on a thin line between rage and submission that made her breathless. She didn't want to review her psyche. Her nights felt empty and quiet, but she couldn't stop thinking about whether Julian's carelessness could be seen as neglect or betrayal.

One very dark afternoon, while she was sorting through his medicine, she found his secret stash of painkillers hidden in an old shoebox. A familiar tremor ran through her body. The bold letters on the bottles screamed, "Don't care." She felt a chill run down her spine as she put the pieces together: he had been hoarding them and maybe even thinking about saying goodbye on purpose. The carefully lined rows of empty pill bottles were proof of choices she thought would change three lives forever. She felt something dark brewing inside of her in the box's shadow.

The line between caring and controlling got blurry. In a fleeting moment, she questioned herself: was it empathy or a desire to control his story? Her heart raced as she thought about how easy it would be for her to become vindictive. For every little thing that made her angry, there was rage that came from feeling weak. She navigated through these thoughts with haunts of Julian's whispered fears, murmurs of worthlessness that echoed in her mind. There remained this constant battle, where compassion stretched against flares of betrayal.

Mary started to make plans in this state of mind. The story she wanted to tell about Julian's death became clear. She wanted to tell a story about his fight and victory, as if she could finally take it back. What would it mean for her if the facade got tighter around her? Would the memories and poetry of their shared past fade into nothing? Or was there something else that would cast a shadow over her carefully crafted professional story that she desperately wanted to keep clean?

The weight of her problem settled heavily on her as she sat with her head in her hands. Could she make money off of a sad story? Would she be a hero in his tragedy or just a scapegoat if things had gone differently? Others had turned Julian's life into a story, and she was afraid of what would happen to her if he chose to end it himself. Could being professional enough help her avoid the cycle of public scrutiny? As she struggled with her feelings, one thought became clear: the truth was unclear, and she had to find her way through the murkiness.

Detective Byrne leaned forward and narrowed her eyes as she stared at Sloane Porter. It felt like her stare could cut through stone. The room was tense, and the smell of old paper and coffee filled the air. Byrne's voice was calm, but there was something sharper about it that made it sound like a lie could break the fragile calm that was left.

"Did you know about the blackmail, Ms Porter?" she asked, keeping a close eye on Sloane's face for any sign of hesitation. Every blink or twitch could have been a crack in the armour.

Sloane sat still, her hands folded neatly on the cold metal table between them. Her face was calm, maybe too calm, like an actor who had mastered the role but was careful not to overdo it. The faint hum of the fluorescent lights above seemed to echo her steady breathing, but Byrne sensed something beneath the surface: a guardedness that didn't quite reach the eyes. The question weighed heavily on Sloane, but she didn't show any signs of the turmoil that was probably going on beneath her polished surface.

Byrne noticed the subtle way Sloane's fingers clenched briefly beneath the table, then relaxed, a silent betrayal of tension she fought hard to hide. It was the kind of small act that said more than words could say. There was an unspoken secret burning beneath the surface. Sloane's denial was calm and collected, but it made the room feel strange, like a shadow was hiding just out of sight. For a moment, Byrne wondered if the truth was always meant to play second fiddle to the story being sold and whether Sloane was selling it best of all.

Mila's fingers trembled slightly as she stared at her phone, her eyes darting between the screen and the dark room around her. The message she was about to send felt heavy, almost physical in her hand, like holding a lead weight. Her mind raced with thoughts: betrayal, regret, a desperate need for the truth to come out, and she knew every word had to cut straight to the core. Finally, after taking a deep breath, she typed out a short, honest message. The words came up on the screen, heavy with the feelings she couldn't hold back anymore.

Mila was signalling the start of a reckoning; she couldn't take it back with that small, shaky act. The message she sent was simple, but it had everything she couldn't say out loud. She wrote it down, and I read it. We need to talk right now, or I'll tell everyone. No detail, no explanation—just those three sentences, packed with her urgent demand for honesty. Every second that passed felt like an eternity, and her heart beat loudly in her ears. The silence that followed was worse than any confrontation; it hovered, thick and unspoken, promising that something was going to break. Mila knew what was at stake: if Julian didn't answer, she would have to do something about it herself, putting everything on the line to get rid of her doubts or reveal her secrets.

As she waited, her toes curled into the carpet and her stomach tightened with excitement. Minutes felt like hours. Then came the first answer, a brief message that made her shiver. Julian answered with calmness that seemed planned, "What do you mean? We're not going back there." His tone was cool and distant, as if he had practised how to avoid the question. The digital silence grew again, full of things that weren't said. Mila felt the walls closing in. She thought of all the reasons he might not want to talk to her: was he really hiding something, or was she wrong to be brave enough to confront him? Each new message from Julian seemed to weigh less like a plea for honesty and more like an ominous warning.

She knew that Julian was a master of control, that behind his polished words was a man who could manipulate every situation to his advantage. Mila, on the other hand, had gone too far. It wasn't just an invitation to talk; it was a challenge. Even though her voice was silent on the screen, it was full of betrayal and a desperate need for a solution. She was ready to go public and tell her story if he didn't open up. She was ready to deal with whatever happened next. The question was whether or not she could still trust him. Did she even want to? Or was her choice to send that message already going to kill her?

She stared at the blinking cursor, waiting for the next answer. She knew that the present was the time when everything could change. A single message from Julian might bring clarity or chaos; either way, Mila understood that silence was no longer an option. Her fingers shook as they hovered over the screen, just like her voice and heart did in that empty room. Every second she waited seemed to make her fears worse: that her confession might start a storm she couldn't handle or that Julian might finally tell everything, and she wouldn't be ready. But she knew she couldn't go back. She had to see this through because staying quiet now would only make the dark thoughts in her head worse.

Finally, the answer came. Julian's words were few but heavy, as if he were carefully picking each letter. He wrote: "Talk now."

The fact that it was so simple calmed her down, but it also sent her mind racing with new questions. Was this a peace deal or a trap? Was this the end of the game, or did he finally take her threat seriously? Mila took a deep breath and felt the weight of her choice settle in her chest. She typed back slowly and carefully: "We need to see each other in person. No screens. It's all about trust."

Her voice held more than just her words; it also held her hope, her fear, and her suspicion. Now, everything depended on what happened next, on that fragile exchange that would determine whether trust could be rebuilt or if the truth was already lost to the shadows.

Detective Byrne looked at the last text message Julian

Vane had sent with a frown on her face. The harsh words had a quiet sense of urgency that suggested there was more to the lie than met the eye. As she reread the message, the corners of her mouth tightened. His tone sounded almost casual, but the words were clearly cold, as if fear was sewn into bravado. What looked like a cry for help was actually full of hidden threats and motives that weren't clear at first glance.

Byrne couldn't shake the feeling that this message wasn't just the last words of a troubled author. It felt more like a spark of something much darker—a weave of desperation that was pushing her to look deeper. Every letter seemed important, and every punctuation mark could be a hint. Julian appeared to be conversing with a person who both required caution and was under his control. She contemplated the intricacy of his message and the multitude of enigmas concealed within this man's ancient manuscripts.

Byrne started to see shadows of blackmail in her mind as she isolated the mysterious phrases and looked at the context around them. She thought of the people who had been hurt by greed and jealousy before her, people she had met while looking into motives that were as different as the people behind them. Byrne could feel the fight coming at 3 PM like a clock ticking in her gut.

The whispers of hidden agendas got louder with every minute, and she could feel the excitement building in her chest. She could feel the tension as she put the pieces together: someone was controlling the story, and Julian was just a pawn in this sick game. The threat of blackmail hung over her findings like a storm cloud ready to burst. Everything would likely come together at this meeting, unveiling motives and hidden truths that had been accumulating and were now irreversible. The tension surrounded her, and it got stronger as the seconds went by. Who would be at the meeting at 3 PM? And what new information would come to light from the dark corners of her investigation?

CHAPTER FOURTEEN

THE PARTY PREP

(2:30 PM)

Mary stepped out of the hospital doors and paused for a moment in the sharp cleanliness of that place, feeling as if she were in a sliding cocoon. The remnants of antiseptic and hospital-engineered smells under her nose combined oddly with the cool, late afternoon air brushing her face. Sunset now; the shadows seem heavier and longer than they should if life had any warmth at all. She tightened her coat more around her, not just to keep warm but as a silent shield against everything that awaited outside those walls. The noise of traffic off in the distance and the murmuring of patients and staff dwindled away, but her senses were very alert, too sharp for the oppressiveness of these last few hours inside.

For a while the drive through town was quiet, but then she became swamped with many thoughts. The streets were narrower than Mary remembered and full of impatient drivers and cyclists weaving in and out. Each turn and changing of lights made the journey like a string of questions left unasked from her brush with sterility. Everything was planned properly for the party coming up: the order the courses should be in, when speeches were scheduled to happen and even which way seats were arranged. Yet there was still a heaviness she couldn't shake here. Like a prayer on her lips: the name of that caterer. Somehow food made well and perfect would help silence the chaos in her brain.

She remembered guests staring at her with these faces – people whose cheeks she had held through many years of happy and sad times with Julian. They wanted not just an occasion; they wanted to leave behind an image, a final truth so clear that once penned in artfully, no one could contest it. What made the party flawless was not just the food or the place. It must also control a story that was so fragile that a bad look or whispered rumour would break it. Her hands tightened on the wheel without her knowing it, Mary. The flowers, the music, and the wines she had decided on all served as part of the story she wanted to tell the world. Although the official records give Julian's death as a natural cause, the party tonight was really meant to cover the heart-soaring anxiety she felt. It was the final, fluid movement in the play that only she knew the script for.

Finally she reached the caterer's shopfront. It lay between a florist and bookshop in a street where polished brass reflected hints of greenery. Mary parked, then sat still for a moment as the engine ticked quietly away and she let herself breathe out. Inside the car, the air was laden with the smell of fluorescent lights from the hospital and years' worth of hidden worries. When she pushed open the door, the low murmur of talk and rich smell of roasting meats with fresh herbs in them were like sweet relief. The caterer smiled at her with an air of excellent discretion one would expect in a serious event such as this, even though no one had told him anything yet. At that moment Mary thought: the present is a time for planning and precision. She set out to recover control of herself even as the world outside seemed set on pulling all her best efforts apart. As they went over the menu again, Mary's mind wandered. The dish one picked had to be right—nothing forceful or that would displace the delicate balance of peace she was trying to maintain now.

It was also not only palatability that mattered, but memories, tradition, and lies that would sustain guests long after the last glass had been raised. Warm colours are for the air, and roasted lamb with rosemary on the bottom is for tradition. Then a salad with mixed greens that provided a cleansing, bitter palate and some sweet vinaigrette to clear off any lingering flavours from your mouth. And dessert; it looked like art but tasted of memories gone by. The caterer put Mary in the picture about when service would start, and she could almost hear staff's movements choreographed to some unseen beat.

The caterer assured Mary that every step of the evening would proceed seamlessly, serving as a fertile ground for truths that were impossible to express directly. As we moved away from the caterers, the sun had set even lower, leaving town in bluish twilight. The streets seemed quieter now, but the tension within Mary did not lift. She gritted her teeth as if keeping her breath. The party was supposed to mark a joyful turning point, a chance to draw a cloak over stories and erase doubts beneath a smooth etiquette of all imagery. Yet the shadows of the hospital, so many unspoken secrets and the fragile threads of memory tightly strung inside her chest reminded her that no matter how perfect an occasion was, it could only muddy the surface and simplify the complexities beneath it. Occasionally the silence as a particular mood between words means more than the words themselves.

As Sloane reached for her phone, her hand shook a little. The screen showed an unanswered call. Every time she called Julian, her heart raced faster, and her fingers pressed the buttons harder and harder. The only sounds in the flat were the refrigerator's soft hum and the sound of traffic outside. Her mind raced through the choices: had he seen the message, or was he ignoring her again? She could almost hear the static of anticipation, which was so loud in her ears that it sounded like a clock ticking louder and louder with each ring.

There was a strange echo in her head, and every call that went unanswered sounded like a hollow drum, sending her a message she wouldn't accept. Julian was usually on time or at least got back to people. The silence now felt wrong; it was thick and heavy, and it was making her chest hurt as her hope turned into worry. She put the phone back to her ear, and her breath caught in her throat. The line stopped, and there was static crackling. Then it went to the dull, empty voicemail. The voice message that should have made her feel better or at least explained things was just a series of beeps. It was a dead end that made her feel worse.

She felt sick as the mental walls she was trying to build fell down, letting panic rise that she couldn't control. What if something had happened? He might have been hurt or worse. Her mind pulled her into vivid, unsettling images—Julian lying unconscious, bleeding, or trapped somewhere she couldn't reach. In her mind, the sterile hallway went on and on, and each thought was more frantic than the last. Every second that went by felt heavier, as if time had slowed down just to make her feel worse. The phone stayed quiet, and the silence of his voice was louder than any words could be.

Sloane tried to stay calm even though she was getting more and more panicked. She felt helpless. She held the device tightly, and her knuckles turned white. Her mind raced through all the things that could be going on—if Julian wasn't answering, maybe he was ignoring her on purpose or even avoiding her altogether. A harsh voice in her head told her to stay calm, but the fear quickly drowned it out. The metallic taste of anxiety stayed on her tongue, a bitter reminder that she was losing control.

The silence, which had been a background worry, now felt like a trap closing around her, getting tighter with each unanswered ring. At that moment, every picture and every doubt came together to form one overwhelming truth: something was very wrong. The walls of her controlled world seemed to close in, and the phone in her hand suddenly felt too heavy to hold. Her once-clear and sharp mind was now in chaos, doubting every little thing about her relationship with Julian. Did he plan this? Was he hiding, hurt, or had he just decided to cut her and everyone else out of his life? As she stared at the dead screen, waiting for a sign that wouldn't come, the uncertainty threatened to swallow her whole. Her heart pounded against her chest, each beat echoing the hollow aching within her.

As Mila drove along the winding roads, her mind raced faster than the car. She gripped the steering wheel tighter. The smell of petrol and the sweet smell of grasslands filled the air. It was a strange contrast to the storm that was brewing inside her. As she drove, her anxiety grew with each mile. She had been going over the words in her head over and over again, letting the phrasing shape her intent and drown out the guilt that was eating at her chest. She spoke softly, as if the sound of her voice could make her more determined.

"I didn't mean to do it; it just happened."

Her voice shook with the weight of her secret, even though she was in her car. The cool breeze that came in through the slightly cracked window didn't do much to cool off the heat that was building up in her stomach. She pictured the moment she walked into Julian's house, where the sunlight spilt like gold paint on the wooden floors. What would she say to Mary, his wife? Would Mary be able to hear the tremor in her voice? Would she look into her eyes and see the truth shining through? Mila imagined their fight, a shaky back-and-forth of accusations and defences, with long pauses full of things that weren't said.

With each breath, her fear grew stronger, but with each exhale, she seemed to fight those fears off for a short time. She was getting ready for a performance, but the stakes were higher than any words could say. When she got to Julian's house, the shadows moved around her, just like her thoughts did. She could already picture the scene: the assembled faces, the weight of her guilt weaving through the air, becoming palpable. At that moment, all she wanted to do was let go of the stress that had built up around her, but she would need to be more careful with her words than she had planned. She could speak and twist the truth just enough to stay out of the spotlight, which could change her fate and maybe even the fate of others. At that moment, every breath she took would be important.

Detective Byrne leaned back in her chair. The soft hum of the light above her desk made the crime scene photos and notes that were all over her desk look pale. The room smelt slightly like old coffee and paper, a smell that was so common that it felt like part of the background noise in investigations like this. She ran her finger along the edge of a ripped piece of fabric that was taped to the file. She thought it was Mary's jacket, and the threads were a little frayed, which is the kind of detail that is easy to miss but not for Byrne. It was clear that everything here was put together with a purpose; it was too exact and planned to be random. The living room was empty now, which was strange because there was no sign of Mary inside. The silence was thick and heavy, like the house itself was waiting for the next piece to arrive.

Byrne squinted as she looked at the faint footprints near

the back door. They were clearly Mila's shape in the dust and wood floor. She understood the timing. Mary had just left, probably to run an errand or go to the doctor, the kind of thing that could pull her away from this fragile home life. Mila, on the other hand, was running towards the house, her nerves making every move she made feel like it was going to hurt. Byrne thought about how Mila's steps would slow down once she crossed the threshold, weighed down by the heavy secret she was carrying and the guilt she felt for what she had done. The differences between the wife and the lover were like a taut wire ready to snap.

The wife was calm and collected, while the lover was full of raw need. From where she was, Byrne could see the small signs that made the difference between being absent and being excited. The clock in the kitchen kept ticking, and each second sounded louder in the quiet room. The corners smelt faintly of antiseptic, and the sharper smell of spilt whisky on the floor—Julian's last treat—mixed with it. Byrne's mind filled in the gaps, from Mary's orderly departure to Mila's unsteady and reckless return. The house was no longer just a place where a man had passed away. It was a stage for a fight that was yet to come, and each player was unknowingly moving closer to the edge of revelation. Byrne could sense the tension in the air as the pieces moved closer together, promising more than just discovery but also a clash of truth, lies, and desperate survival.

Byrne could see the pattern clearly: Mary had slipped away without a sound, leaving only traces in glassware and worn leather. Mila was the storm coming, and there was no way to stop it. Byrne thought that the tension would rise sharply when the lover came in, carrying both guilt and defiance with her. Byrne's fingers hovered over the notes as she made mental maps of the stories each woman might tell if they had to explain where they had been and what they knew. There was a clear rhythm to everything, like the steady beat of a story being rewritten in real time, full of doubt and secret glances.

Byrne's eyes moved to the window, where the light outside had started to fade, creating long shadows that surrounded the room. Every flicker of shadow made the details clearer: a chair that had been turned over, a glass with a faint lipstick mark, and a countertop that had been scrubbed quickly. Byrne could only see the mosaic made up of all the small signs on top of each other. She knew how important timing, movement, and stillness were.

The wife was outside, calm and detached, keeping her distance from the chaos. The lover was on her way, nervous and unstable, with more than just herself inside the walls of that strange, quiet house. Byrne could almost hear the quiet prayers or hurried excuses each one would make, as well as the hidden truths that could break at the slightest hint of a crack. Byrne thought that this was the moment—the calm before the inevitable fight—when the real story started to come apart. The empty rooms echoed secrets, and Byrne's mind raced after the lines she couldn't see yet but thought were there: who left first, who came back last, and what each person wanted to hide or show. Every little thing was important. The worn-out carpet had threadbare spots, the air smelt faintly of lavender even though there was a lot of tension, and the only cigarette in the ashtray was still burning. Byrne knew that when Mila got there, the atmosphere would be tense, unstable, and open to either confession or accusation. Before the storm hit, Byrne sharpened her focus. She knew that the truth was more like a moving shadow than a fixed point, and she needed to catch it before it got away again.

CHAPTER FIFTEEN

THE CONFRONTATION

(3:00 PM)

Julian Vane felt as though silence enveloped his study. The room was filled with the wan light of late afternoon that forced its way through heavy black curtains, throwing long shadows over the littered desk and shelves strewn with worn books and yellowing manuscripts. The sound of silence was overwhelming, all pierced only by the low drone of far-off streets outside the closed window. The room was deadly silent and still, not a sign of life or movement to break the silence that lent it an eerie chill, as if the very walls were holding their breath. The stillness outside Julian's door heightened the tension, suggesting an invisible presence lurking just beyond the wood's edge.

The muffled voices of investigators waft through the thick door, their sound dampened but insistent, packed tight like an ongoing puzzle. The smell of old paper, mixed with the stale scent of coffee long gone cold, hung in the room. It was a smell of years of late-night writing, of key moments struck in inspiration combined with the exhaustion following. Occasionally, the muted click-clack of shoes on wood and the gentle rustling of papers were audible reminders that life was happening right on the other side of the door. But there was no one entered, and the silence became more oppressive within, laying itself against the walls of the room like something unuttered clamouring to be heard.

Beyond the door hung a multitude of questions that weighed on investigators as they combed through every detail in an effort to recreate a chain of events. The loudness of their voices now, between brief periods of strained silence, also betrayed how far they failed to comprehend that the very scene might all be a grand illusion. Every item in the room — whether it was wrinkled papers strewn across the bed, an uncompleted glass of water or neatly arranged writing utensils — offered clues and contradictions. The air was dense with a sense of expectancy but not stained in any way by Mary or Julian. Each moment passed with a gnawing realisation that something essential was eluding her, something that could turn everything around once it saw the light of day.

The scene outside the study was no less calm. The agents' whispers murmured in the background as the house around bristled with a silent commotion. The vague smell of fresh tears, combined with the odour of burnt toast from breakfast several hours before, still hovered in the air, a physical manifestation of the emotional pressure that was resting upon them all. The house was quiet, but the stress was just hovering there like a needle that wouldn't drop. Each member there had worries of their own, fears that the truth, so harsh and confronting, might never fully be known. The silence in the room seemed to conceal secrets while simultaneously trapping everyone's internal conflicts, poised to be revealed.

Which is why Mary's absence from the scene was notable. It was not just the physical distance; it was that huge void she created. Her seat was there, her belongings, as if she had simply slipped out in the mayhem. Nobody could locate her; nobody could quite work out where she had gone or what she was thinking. She should have been Julian's wife, but now she appeared to be no more than a ghost hovering on the other side of silence and invisibility, which nonetheless filled the emptied spaces that her not being there caused. That hollowness said everything about her state of mind—a cocktail of guilt, shame, and something deeper that she couldn't or wouldn't grapple with just yet.

It felt as though the house, for all its enforced calm, was holding its breath in her absence. Her serenity clashed with the frenzy of the probe. They had all known she was tight with Julian; it was difficult to pretend that they didn't see her being cold now. She had been a fixture in Julian's life—a stable source, or so it seemed. But today her vanishing pointed to secrets she'd sooner have escaped. It was more than just her missing flesh and blood, a reminder caught in the lack of space when they'd all gather together. Whatever she kept concealed, whatever whispers her silence exposed, the truth would finally be revealed. But not today. The house still held onto its secrets too tightly to confess the mystery.

Julian's voice is thin and unsteady, but there is still a

lot of weight behind it after decades of telling tales. The weak speaker's voice is like a ghostly whisper, mirroring the tension that had clenched up all of our throats just moments before everything was different. It seems as if he chose those syllables meticulously, because he knew they were the last parts of his soul. He's speaking about love, betrayal and the endless hunger for legacy — but there is a more sinister motive behind his confessions.

The listener can picture the scene of their last fight vividly, and the tension is dense as steam on a window. It's not hard to imagine Sloane attempting to rationalise what they discussed as her stomach churns with concern. She knew that he was too smart, too adroit at getting what he wanted. Now, as he records his last words, that same sense of unease returns. It is part of his enigmatic and frightening method — the way he tells queer stories to reveal a truth. Sloane understands that his passing won't simply be a goodbye; it's an orchestrated event of chaos, one that will make his death a work of art.

In her darkened office, Mary is frozen in place with a combination of fear and fascination as she stares at the recorder. It's kind of like a heartbeat every time that recording light is winking, with all the elided weight of things that could potentially be found. She knows that pressing play could destroy everything she's worked to build: her life, her marriage and perhaps the personal reputation she has cultivated. But the idea of leaving it unacknowledged is gnawing away at her, and fueling her fears and doubts.

The silence is electric, filled with her anxiety in the moment as she struggles to determine what to do. She thinks about how Julian's health was deteriorating, but what disturbs her most are the petty fights and bitterness that had seeped between them. The guilt grows stronger every second that passes. Should she hear his last words and perhaps learn things that she must face? Or should she conceal the evidence and not care what may come of it? The battle in her mind illustrates that she loves him but needs to look out for herself. The situation demonstrates the difficulty she faces trying to be good in a world where love and manipulation often do battle.

Mila arrived at Julian's house just as the rain stopped. There were still wet leaves and the strong smell of wet earth on the street. Her hands shook on the wheel, and her heart raced with a mix of fear and need. The ancient brick home appeared to be vanishing in the gloomy light of the low, heavy sky above. She went outside, and the sound of her feet hitting the broken pavement was too loud for the quiet night. The air was heavy, not just because it was humid, but also because they hadn't talked to each other about all the things they wanted to. The memories of their last fight still hurt her chest like knives.

The cold air that came in through the walls mixed with the faint smell of smoke and old cologne as Mila went inside. The hallway didn't have much light, and the corners were dark, which made them look long and strange. She looked at the old wallpaper and the prints that were all over the floor. The prints on the floor were little reminders of the life they had together before it fell apart. She felt a mix of anger, guilt, and fear every second that went through her mind. There was more than just a fight waiting for her on the other side of the door. It was the end of something that had been falling apart for a long time.

Julian was already in the living room when she got there. He was standing by the window with his back to her. The streetlights outside made one side of his face look dark. He didn't say anything or turn around right away. Then his voice came, calm but sharp, and he said something that hurt more than any fight. He told her he would never leave Mary, not now or in the future. The words were like ice. The way he talked made the room feel smaller and the air thicker, as if the walls were closing in on her. His laugh was quiet and empty, and it didn't reach his eyes. It sounded more like pain mixed with anger. That laughter, which was a bitter way to hide her pain, made Mila's anger turn into something fierce and desperate.

Her anger was like a living thing that pulled her closer to

him. Words came out quickly and sharply—fear, anger, and accusations—until she pushed him. It seemed like the movement caught both of them off guard. Julian fell back and then caught himself on the edge of the couch. Everything stopped for a moment, and then his head hit the wooden armrest with a sickening crack. She would rather not admit it, but the sound was louder in her ears than she wanted it to be. Julian was slumped there, blinking his eyes. He looked either shocked or confused. The fight had turned into something dark and real, and all of a sudden, the room didn't seem like a good place to argue anymore. She stepped back, her heart racing and panic rising like a wave she wasn't ready for.

Julian's hand shook as he reached for the side table and looked for a small pill bottle. He gripped the glass with his fingers, which shook as if the smallest movement could break him completely. Then, just as she was about to cry and her breath caught, he said it in a sharp, quiet voice: "Go away." The command was more like a wound; it broke the thick silence and told her that there was no going back, regardless of what this night had turned into. Mila's mind was racing, and she could taste fear in her mouth. She took a step back and didn't say anything else. The door clicked shut behind her, and she ran into the cold night, leaving the dark behind.

Detective Byrne was hunched over her crowded desk, waiting at rapt attention for the grainy footage on her laptop to play through. The neighbour's surveillance camera had recorded a short interval that appeared unremarkable at first blush, but Byrne knew better. The little timestamp shifting in the corner hovered just above the tiny figure of Mila, a blur moving so fast you could barely see her flash onto our porch at exactly 2:58 p.m. She seemed rushed, almost anxious, shoulders hunched as if she wanted nothing more than to duck out of sight into Julian's house. Byrne never took his eyes off the monitor as a dark shadow—Mila zipping along and then, in less than a blink, looooong gone, shooting out of sight at 3:17 p.m. Those minutes, seconds really, were heavy with unspoken tension. It was not just a matter of Mila's timing; it was also about what those eighteen minutes hid under the ordinary glare of the camera lens.

Watching as Byrne rewound the footage, she couldn't help but visualise what led up to one of those off-screen moments. The camera had recorded only Mila's arrival and departure before heading back to Canberra, and Byrne knew that less than twenty minutes could contain all manner of secrets. Had Mila come here on purpose, or had she fled an unknown force? What is it that she had seen or heard that called for such expeditiousness? Each wary look, each sack-like step was the picture of a person attempting to slink into hiding and conceal secrets that might destroy her innocence — or reveal guilt. Byrne's mind stored acorns of suspicion: how Mila fussed with her hands, clutched her bag tightly and started breathing more heavily as she prepared to leave. All of this information hinted that the arrival and departure of Mila were not isolated random acts but somehow part of a bigger, more complicated mosaic yet to be revealed.

The scene changes from the tape to Byrne, who is now paying close attention to the timestamps, her intuition intensifying as she looked at each clip. She stopped at the exact moment Mila's figure arrived, seeing that she moved a little slower, which may mean she was afraid or unsure. The tick-tock of the clock created a feeling that time was precious—minute by minute slipping away chances or evidence. Byrne's eyes followed the seconds in her mind as she set out to piece together the timeline like a jigsaw puzzle. The quiet in the room was heavy with what was about to happen. Now this seemingly so mundane ground and cast-off suddenly felt like crucial parts to a puzzle only she had been able to glimpse. It was obvious: Mila's quick, calculated steps had intersected a time frame—a sliver of opportunity that just might lead to what actually occurred in those crucial minutes beyond Julian's death.

Byrne knew that such camera-ready flashes frequently obscured deeper truths. She knew that Mila's dislike of the other people might be interpreted as nervousness due to fear or guilt. Was Mila caught in a web of her own creation? Maybe she was spooked and left because he didn't want to misinterpret what her actions might suggest; who knows? Those eighteen minutes meant something, like a pulse whispering secrets in the stillness. Byrne's experience taught her that this short window was a trigger point — part of the modern-day dance where something can either be the key that unlocks everything or deepen the mystery. Any little thing, no matter how small, indicated an unseen narrative. The task was to translate the running about of Mila and to find out what had happened in that twinkling manner. Somewhere in there, Byrne was certain, lay the truth that would change everything she thought she knew about the night Julian died. The notion excited her, as she examined more footage with the hope of extracting the secrets hidden in those vital seconds.

Believing she may be on to something big, Byrne decided to analyse the footage frame by frame. She kept track of how dark it was getting, the shifting shadows indicating time of day, and where Mila's figure was in relation to travelling. Small tells — the fast glance over her shoulder or the subtle brush of her bag —

were big. As she had thought to herself, Mila's sudden leaving was not a coincidence; there must have been something that compelled her to depart so hurriedly. Byrne had explored both scenarios: Everything from whether or not Mila ran away on her own to "Was she forced or was she pushed?" The timorous tremor of the man in every movement betrayed guilt or terror. Byrne's instincts told her that where Mila had gone was a critical piece of the puzzle: perhaps it held the key to what happened in Julian's last few hours. But the camera could not tell her everything. She had to look deeper into why Mila happened to show up at exactly 2:58 and flee at precisely 3:17 and what she left behind in those few minutes that would help her turn the course of her investigation forever.

Chapter Sixteen

THE GAP

(3:17 PM – 4:25 PM)

The caterer's office was poorly lit and smelt strongly of fresh herbs and spices that had been there for a long time. She felt the weight of the last few hours on her chest as she stepped up to the counter, which was covered in bills, receipts, and half-empty coffee cups. Every piece of paper she glanced at made her think of the well-planned alibi she was trying to put together in the minutes before Julian's death. She ran her fingers over the edges of the receipts, and each one brought back a memory: the sound of laughter at the party, the clinking of glasses, and Julian's magnetism that drew people to him like moths to a flame.

She scribbled down the times and other details when she discovered the proper papers. This helped her remember how long she had been at the event, when she had left, and where she had gone after that. Mary needed this not just for the investigation but also to feel better. The caterer stared at her with a suspicious look, but he didn't say anything. She couldn't blame him; it was a long night. She felt her heart accelerate when she thought of the chaos that had happened behind the flawless social facade. To everyone else, she was merely a doctor, a wife, and a lady who had lost her husband in a terrible way. But beneath that mask was a lady attempting to get her tale back, making an honest story out of the lies that Julian had left behind.

It felt like the drive home would never end, as everything outside transformed into a swirl of colours and shapes. Mary's thoughts were suddenly broken by the sight of Mila's automobile rushing away from Julian's estate, its tyres screeching on the asphalt. In that short time, she felt an odd mix of things. Her stomach hurt because she was angry, confused, and a little scared. What made Mila so eager to leave? Did she know something? Mary tried to forget about it, but the dark clouds that were building over her heart wouldn't go away.

Everything felt different when I returned home at 4:30 PM. She thought of the storm that was coming when she saw shadows hiding in the corners of the well-lit rooms. She tried to fit together the pieces of what had happened to her recently: the catering office, Julian's final breath, and now Mila's desperate escape. Everything was starting to mix together into a confused web of falsehoods and memories that weren't quite right. Mary had found out about the mess that was Julian's life and the secrets it carried while trying to be helpful. She got ready for the storm that was coming and recognised that the alibi she thought would protect her might perhaps be what kept her tethered to the truth that was coming.

It can be good to keep a comprehensive record of where you are and what you say when things go awry. If you write down where you went, it can help you stay grounded throughout a chaotic event. This can help you put together the fragmented timeline and keep yourself safe when the story and the truth don't match up.

Sloane's small, filthy office was full of silent stress in the late afternoon. It was the only place she could get away from the nonstop noise of literary meetings and publishing deadlines for a few hours. The sunlight entering through the dirty blinds formed lengthy shadows on the old carpet and stacks of papers. It was close to 4:25. The noise of the city outside sounded far away, like a secret that was just out of grasp of these four walls. At this specific moment, every second appeared to lengthen, and the air seemed tight as if the clock's sluggish tick was measuring time not just in minutes but also in silent, unspoken pressure. The quiet was so heavy that it felt like it was choking her. The area didn't feel like an office; it felt more like a trap that stopped secrets and her thoughts from calming down.

People could feel Sloane's absence, like a hole in the room that made them question what was going on. There were neatly piled documents with Julian Vane's fading signature on them on one side of the chair, which was moved under the desk. It seemed like she had softly left, leaving behind an unseen trail of tension that poured from the pages like ink on water. People who knew what to look for could observe a slight difference in the way the light hit where she had last sat, which showed that she had left quickly. The story she wanted to tell had already started long before anyone came into this room. It made Julian's death look like a sad suicide by an artist. The need to stop a termination email after finding Julian's body wasn't only about money; it was also about controlling the tale and turning chaos into a legacy.

Sloane didn't merely leave to run errands or take a break; she departed on purpose to get away from a spot where Julian had been manipulating her. She seemed calm on the outside, but on the inside she was a maelstrom of fear, loss, and a cold calculation that hadn't yet transformed into despair. She felt her fingers quiver a little as she thought of the stolen manuscript that Mila would use to blackmail her and the secret voice recorder that she thought she had. The tension built even more when the visuals went beyond what could be seen—the small tightening of her jaw, the momentary flash of vulnerability before a practised mask took its place; a performance prepared for viewers who might never comprehend how much she cared about the subject.

Every move she made was a hint, and every blink was a sign of a war inside her that she wasn't ready to talk about. There was no emptiness in her absence; it was a charged void full of unspoken accords and facts that had not yet been disclosed. There were supposed to be many participants in the manipulation around Julian's death, but Sloane's part was the most perilous. She could either save a faltering brand or let it sink. The ticking of the clock in that small room brought her back to reality. It reminded her that time was running out—not just for Julian Vane, but also for the version of the tale she was fighting so hard to safeguard.

The room seemed to be holding its breath, waiting for her to come back, but Sloane was still lost in her thoughts somewhere else. This absence was full with everything she wasn't saying: the stress of going bankrupt, the shame of betraying her loyalty, and the desperate hope that the story she put together would hold up under inspection. Her silence spoke more than words could. It was a gentle way of saying that the strongest person is sometimes the one who isn't present.

The home feels heavier than it should in the late afternoon light. Shadows stretch across the old wooden floorboards, making the edges of furniture look softer and creating a lovely, flickering darkness over everything. The air inside smells like spilt coffee and old paper, which are Julian's most valued possessions: his unending manuscripts. The quiet is almost deafening, save for the faint sound of a clock ticking in the distance, which seems to count the minutes Julian has already spent out of reach. The house seems to be holding its breath, waiting for something that might never happen: the sound of Mila's footsteps echoing down the halls again.

For now, the plot feels hollow and disturbing without Mila. Mila's leaving is more than just her going away; it makes a quiet chorus of unanswered questions. The last time anyone saw her, she was in a hurry, her face was sweaty, and she was shivering as she hurried away with something in her hands. The disarray she left behind makes it seem like there are secrets that no one knows about. Every look and every strange thing she does in a hurry suggest that her life is just as convoluted as Julian's, but for a very different cause. There are a lot of stories that haven't been told since she left. These stories may never be found, or they may be hiding in the rubble of Julian's last moments.

It seems like the house is holding its breath in the hush, as if it knows what Mila brought with her. The smooth sound of her shoes scraping the porch and the fast sound of her heels hitting wood are gone now. There is a crushing hush instead. Julian's writing desk is a tangle of unfinished manuscripts and crumpled notes, which shows how busy his mind is. The newest bag in the corner, which used to house Mila's medical supplies, makes a slight metallic sound. Now that she's gone, it feels like a planned feature of the house, changing the story and adding to the mystery. Every shade and space appears to hint that she was there for a short time, making it evident that her genuine goals and anxieties are still veiled behind her fast escape.

As darkness falls, the tension rises like a wire that is about to break. When Mila isn't present, the story's cadence changes. It slows down and is full of doubt and overthinking. Did she depart because she was suddenly scared? Or did she decide on purpose to cover her tracks? The chance is in the air, and it's thick enough to eat. Each detail points to a different story, yet none of them match properly. Her fast leave, the dispute with Julian, and the fact that she feels she caused his fall all make her feel guilty—or innocent. The home still whispers her name, telling anybody who wants to know that her part in this bizarre drama isn't ended yet. The ripped-up fabric, the smudged fingerprints, and the thrown-away key are all parts of a broader jigsaw that she left behind.

The idea that Mila's absence might be her way of being quiet—a protest, a shield, or maybe even her last act of control in a situation that was getting out of hand—is the most frightening. Her departure starts a chain reaction that will affect the path of the investigation forever. It forces everyone to face the unknown truth, and there are a lot of questions that are yet unresolved. Did she really care about what would happen to her if she did what she did? Or was she trying to get away from what she saw was a fatal scenario in some way? These questions keep coming up in quiet places, making Mila's absence even scarier. It's a note that hasn't been resolved in a symphony of lies and secrets. The narrative isn't over yet because she hasn't been located, and her motivations for what she did haven't been made apparent. It waits quietly in the dark for the time when it can hear her voice again.

Detective Byrne sat in her dark office, which smelt like old coffee and worn-out notepads. The death of Julian Vane had become a maze, with a 70-minute pause in the middle. That short time between Mila leaving and Mary being there was really important. She watched the security film again, and her brow furrowed as the same scenes repeated over and over. Mila walked out of the fancy building with a determined look on her face and held on to her purse hard. She left behind a sense that was stronger than anything else on the screen.

Byrne then looked over the logs of the conversations. Text messages, phone calls, and time stamps. Mila's frantic call to Sloane only made matters more confusing. What had she learnt in those few seconds that made her feel like she had to act? As Mila moved, every little thing about her became important, and Byrne could feel the atmosphere become more tense. How about Mary? She wasn't just here by chance. It looked like she didn't know the complete story because she showed up only 70 minutes later. It seemed like she was involved in something far more sophisticated than basic timeframes could convey.

By putting the pieces together, Byrne saw how unsure Mila's last moments were. What if she had to leave the building right away because she was scared? Byrne trembled at the notion of what might happen. Mila might have been alive, rushing away from something horrible that was hiding in the dark. What if Mary walked into a place that was already full of Mila's mess? That would make things even more risky for her.

It seemed like every angle was about to tumble. Byrne was curious about how much Mary really knew. Did she walk into a scene that was different, with the air thick with the sounds of terror and fighting? Or maybe she had a bigger role to play in all of this? The women's scepticism was like a tightrope that changed with each new piece of evidence or eyewitness narrative. The mystery continued exciting, and every new twist made Byrne question what she thought she understood about the reality, the reasons behind it, and who the victim and the culprit were.

As the clock ticked, she had a moment of clarity: maybe the solution wasn't in black and white but in the grey spaces. The 70-minute interval was full of stories, each one seeking to grab attention and full of suspense. Because it was so unclear, the case wasn't just an inquiry; it was also an analysis of what people choose, what they are frightened of, and what they are under pressure to do.

THE AUTOPSY

(The Next Day)

Mary stood stiffly in the cold, antiseptic waiting area, where the strong smell of disinfection filled her nose and stuck to the back of her throat. The bright fluorescent lights flickered softly above, casting lengthy shadows on the white walls. A low buzz that sounded like a warning went across the air. She felt like every breath was too loud and every second lasted forever as she waited for someone to tell her what had happened to Julian. The air tasted dry and heavy, and it blended with the slight metallic fragrance that stuck to her skin. This smell reminded her of endings and hospitals, but she remained silent.

Her hands shook in her lap, and her fingers moved over the scratchy fabric of the chair as if they were drawing lines that weren't there. It felt like the spotless room was closing in on her, like a veil that was too tight. A man in a white coat came in after the door opened. It was impossible to determine what he was thinking because his countenance was serious. The words poured out in a cold and professional manner, revealing the findings of the autopsy. Something inside Mary crumbled when she learnt the truth. The autopsy told her things she would rather not hear, things that went against all she hoped for and felt. She felt her heart racing as she struggled to make sense of the cold, harsh truths in front of her.

"That's impossible," she said in a voice so low that it was hard to hear. It rattled like a thread that was about to break. As the weight of denial pressed down on her chest, her skin felt clammy and her face lost colour. Julian's death defied her familiar logic. She wanted to shout, struggle, and dispute the news that sounded so terrible and definitive. Every instinct prompted her to keep him safe and make the story less harsh and more gentle. But the truth of the autopsy was a strong, relentless force that made her choose between what was true and what she wanted to be real.

Sloane sat stiffly in the chilly, sterile hallway of the hospital. The bright fluorescent lights made her nerves tingle.

She put her ear up to the broken speaker on the portable recorder that the forensic team was using and tried hard to hear every word of the pathologist's distant, clinical voice. You could hear people writing, soft beeping, and footsteps that weren't too loud in the background. The chamber smelt like disinfection and metal, and the smell of cleanliness hung in the air like a warning. Everything appeared to slow down as she listened, similar to how the pathologist's voice kept aloof and seemingly disinterested as he talked about the autopsy results in a robotic way. She had imagined this sight, but now that she was there, it felt weird, with the stark reality whispering a sharp reminder of what was at risk.

When Sloane heard the term "narcotics," she looked worried. The word hung in the air like a heavy cloud, unspoken but impossible to miss. She thought about drugs right away since she knew that talking about them could shatter the fragile image she was trying so hard to make for Julian Vane. She realised that even a whiff of drugs would make the tale she sought to control more problematic and potentially ruin her professional reputation. This additional knowledge could shift the story from a tragic death that might have been unavoidable to something worse and more scandalous. She felt the familiar surge of anxiousness as she tightened her grip on her handbag. The medical examiner then discussed the medicines that were found in Julian's body. The words were so heavy that they hurt, reminding her that things weren't as nice and uncomplicated as she wanted them to be.

Sloane's head was whirling as she thought about her options and practiced the scenarios she could describe. She made money by controlling Julian's image, regulating how he appeared in public, and turning his convoluted existence into a story that sold. She heard the term "narcotics" in her head and realised that this could wreck everything. Would the news media pick up on the story and say it was abuse or self-harm? Would fans come to think that medications were to blame for Julian's deterioration instead of normal ageing or illness? She shook her fingers a little as she pondered about what to do next. She realised that reality would be a jumble, with too many doubts and questions to deal with. She could only hope to adjust the story before the facts got out of hand, making the death appear like a natural conclusion or something less scandalous than what the evidence could truly lead to.

As she read the news about the autopsy results, Mila's pulse raced. She had a mix of terror and curiosity in her stomach that made it difficult to breathe. It was like she was trying to put together jigsaw pieces of a world that was too messy to fit together. The article talked about Julian's death in a clinical fashion, identifying various causes, each one scarier than the last. Mila's mind was racing with ideas. She kept thinking about the last few minutes they spent together, trying to make sense of the mess.

The flash of panic made her feel worse and made her think of questions she didn't want to think about. Was what she did connected to what happened to him? Did their fight change things for good? Every time she felt guilty, it hit her harder than the last time. She remembered how keen Julian's eyes were when he told her everything was OK just before she left his house that night. Her recollections were like stepping stones that moved her ahead but sometimes made her stop and think since she was so unsure.

When Mila received the autopsy results, she felt like she was in the middle of a whirlwind of feelings. There was a lot of guilt and not much relief. She didn't like the idea that he had planned his death as part of his art. Could she have overlooked the clues? She remembered their last talk, which was full of true and half-true points. She could feel the tension in the air, like the apprehension that comes before a tragedy or the static charge that arrives before a storm.

She was thinking about several things that didn't make sense: the secret she kept, the manuscript she stole, and the quarrel they had. I doubted myself each time I replayed the same thoughts over and over. It made her tongue taste bittersweet to see Julian laugh and his eyes gleam. Could he have written an ending for both of them, not just for himself? Did he see her as a character in his story, someone who would be in his closing act? As she pondered about this hard truth, her stomach twisted into knots of fear that got worse with every thought she had.

As she started going through her sentiments, she felt like she had to do something right away. The news told her the reality, which made her seem grey. There was ambition, anxiety, and maybe even treachery in how she felt about Julian. The revelation made me feel uneasy. She wanted to stop feeling awful and view herself as simply another person reading the sad drama that was going on around her. But the truth was a lot more complicated. Her thoughts were like a complex maze, with every turn bringing her back to her and the choices she made.

In the days after she heard the news, she wrestled with her thoughts and feelings while life carried on outside. People she knew and friends were buzzing about her, without understanding that there was a lot of craziness going on inside her. The world didn't seem to care about her problems as she went about her regular life. Everything, even the grin of a barista or the laughing of a stranger, felt sharp and made her feel worse during these times.

Occasionally, the turmoil made her feel better. She heard the news about Julian's death and watched how individuals who didn't know him well responded. Their fears were the same as hers, and their queries became hers. But the more she listened, the more she felt like she was in a tale that was happening to her and that she couldn't influence.

Mila understood that as time went on, she couldn't stay stuck in the turmoil. She needed to understand what all of her feelings meant. Facing the reality would be the toughest thing for her to do after Julian died. Every small change in her feelings made her understand more. She had to deal with not just the shame and dread she felt, but also the times when they made things clearer. She had to know that her search for a story might either connect her to his or set her free.

As she went around her flat attempting to sort things out, one thing became clear: she needed to figure out Julian's strange work to properly comprehend her position. She wanted to be more than just a supporting character in his story; she wanted to write her story by figuring out the strands of the story he left behind. This would bring light to the dark regions he left behind.

Detective Byrne sat alone in the dark interrogation room with the autopsy report in front of her, which seemed like a riddle that needed to be solved. Every word she read made her feel worse about the awful reality regarding Julian Vane's death. The thorough toxicological results stood out: Julian had a lot of medications in his system that were against the law. These things were like uninvited guests in his body, which scared him and shocked him. There were no beta-blockers or statins in his system to explain the slow, consistent fall; Mary stated he was taking his heart meds just as prescribed.

There were these medications, and they weren't just a strange medical situation; they were a warning sign. Not the natural way for a heart to fail or a silent accident, as the early theories stated. The investigation revealed a complex mix of medications, including narcotics not prescribed by anyone at the hospital. The toxicologist had warned that the levels were high enough to make it difficult to breathe. These odd compounds made Julian's heart weak, not the sickness.

Byrne let her eyes linger on the details: the mix of opioids, the lack of any medical reason, and the time of intake all plainly pointed away from natural causes. The pattern was not a mistake. The surgical perfection, in fact, suggested that someone had tampered with the evidence or, worse, poisoned the victim on purpose and made it look like a medical event. The chemistry made it evident that there was a plan. The death certificate might say "undetermined" for now, but Byrne knew the incident wasn't just poor luck.

The detective's thoughts raced as she pieced the pieces together. There was a clear reason why someone put these medications in Julian's body. It wasn't just an accidental overdose or a casual error; it was a premeditated, cold act to take advantage of his already poor health. This act of murder was disguised as a disease. The medications were a weapon, and the fact that they were there made it hard to accept that Julian died of natural causes or an accident.

Byrne puzzled about what that meant. The medicines must have come from someone who was close enough to Julian to influence his environment and knew how weak he was but was willing to push him over the edge. The report cut through the chaos of lies and conflicting stories like a scalpel, making it evident that what at first seemed like a difficult puzzle was really a planned murder. The reasoning was stark and clear: a man didn't survive these substances in his blood by luck.

The fixed attitudes changed when they learnt this information. There was no longer any consolation in the explanations that said the person had died naturally after years of illness or that they had made a mistake that led to their death. Medical jargon disguised this as murder, a crime that demanded a swift resolution to prevent any misunderstandings. Byrne could already hear the suspects' claims falling apart because of this proof. Julian's body had the narcotics in it, which was the smoking gun.

THE SECOND SEARCH

Mary watched silently from the door, looking at the policemen as they went around systematically through the room. She had her hands tightly gripped together and in front of her, and even though she had a look that was steady almost to severity above the bandage mask, no one present could fail to see the trembling of her fingers. The sound of the smallest things — the snap of a pen, the crinkle of paper — suddenly became unbearably loud. She breathed rhythmically, trying to control the butterflies in her chest; the calm façade she wore was only a superficial relief from her turmoil. She could feel her nerves tense even more as thoughts raced through her head that she wasn't brave enough to voice: Did they find something? Can this upend everything? As a cardiologist, her work required composure, but here in the silent anarchy of darkness, her body had yielded to that quiet control.

She looked on as the team searched, meticulously removing layers of what appeared to be bloodstained fabric and personal items. Her eyes had landed on a small, wheeled tray holding blood samples and evidence bags

— well, as much of it as she would acknowledge; more than anything else, what she saw were the little flashpoints of hesitation or irritation on their faces. It felt as though each of them understood what was at stake, the very fragile truth fumbling within this mess. And her mind kept returning to how she had let herself become involved in all this, particularly with her search, which now appeared to have been a mistake. A doctor's job was supposed to be understanding the human body, not searching for clues that could incriminate her or bring up unpleasant truths she had hoped were buried.

Watching them, she thought about her own hands — steady during many surgeries but now trembling with another kind of tension. Her gaze fell on the open medical bag she'd pulled out of her closet earlier, its contents immaculately arranged inside; one of those vials wrapped in sterile paper might be what she needed. She had sensed, instinctively somehow, where not to look for narcotics. She had only been looking for a sign of trouble... anything that would explain Julian's rapid slide. But now, doubts seeped in. Or did she truly see nothing, and was there something she couldn't see, something that lent a darker colouration to this already complicated picture? Her brain was attempting to reconcile what she knew of medicines with the pandemonium that was being unleashed around her.

When the small bag of drugs was revealed, the room went quiet. For a moment, everything slowed — the widening of the investigators' eyes, the faint smell of chemicals hanging in the air. Mary's pulse jumped a bit, but her face remained impassive. This was impossible. She was aware that these drugs were not hers. She'd never seen them before and couldn't even tell what they were just by looking. Her brain did not want to believe what her eyes were registering. She hurried to voice her denial, her tone calm but firm:

"Those aren't mine. I don't know how those got here."

Her voice was steady, almost rehearsed, and yet underneath it she felt the weight of truth – this couldn't be an accident, could it? It wasn't like she was involved, was it? But inside, a nagging little worry murmured that she might be more caught up than she was willing to let herself believe.

She already knew how lethal a false lead could be at these instants. She was used to explaining complications in her patients' cases and to defending her reputation. The accusation seemed to hang in the air, thick and heavy. Could she pass off her professional skills as a way of holding back the doubts, or would the very instruments with which her own mind worked betray her?

"I swear I've not seen those drugs," she said and kept her voice steady. "I swear, I have never seen these drugs before. They're not mine."

But in her gut, she knew that denial alone may not be sufficient. There was evidence, and her silence can be seen as complicity. She had to think of some way to persuade herself — and for that matter everyone else — that her own conscience was clear, even if now for the thousandth time she gazed around her with rapid glances at the bag, which seems continually tripping up her feet in a most astonishing manner over this cursed thing anyway — can it be possible?

There was palpable tension in the studio as detectives sifted meticulously through Julian's raunchy belongings. The pristine room seemed frigid, almost dead, filled with every clipped paper and organised folder, yet there was no hint of comfort. They had turned it all into a set for their hunt and their desperate question, the question that could somehow unlock his enigmatic last hours. They worked up an inventory of manuscripts, photographs and letters, sifting through the artefacts left by a life that had only recently flickered out. Every piece they handled had a memory, a shard of Julian's brilliance, but what they were hunting now was more malevolent—something that might rip holes in the delicate web spun about his death.

The silence was broken periodically by the soft rustle of paper and the telling snap of plastic evidence bags. The detectives tramped with a combination of urgency and trepidation, aware of the gravity their assessment would carry. Every detail mattered. The photos tacked to the corkboard evoked both laughter and despair, revealing the range of emotions Julian inspired. But no matter how hard she tried, the real clues were buried too deep, protected by layers of artifice that Julian always wore, like defensive armour. What had occurred in the hours before he died? The quest seemed to be less a search for truth than a retrieval of some fragile thing, the shy little sister to tru-enfance.

In Sloane's absence the psychological atmosphere of the room became solid, at least to Mary. She stood at the edge of the circle, watching detectives work and feeling that same gnawing fear beneath her calm surface. Every casual shared gaze between the designates made her feel as if a piece of glass had grated through her shield's calm and shredded it, leaving raw edges. Julia's thoughts were darting, each momentary thought darker than its predecessor, pushing her to wonder what role she herself had played in this sorry story. What would they find? Would her crimes, her humiliations, be exposed for the world to know?

Mary's heart pounded, and her misery intensified as the systematic search continued with no end in sight. The study, a place of laughter and quiet dreams, now became an arena of interrogation and doubt. The walls started to press and squeeze on her, pressing the memory of the way she had fought with Julian's slow decay to form a featureless smudge against them, but it was the same old battles because there's nothing so oppressive as being a supportive wife. Now, as she approached the digging investigators—and, more to the point, as their prodding questions reverberated in her head—it was all coming apart at last: the fragile string of narrative that she had done her best to steer. The pressure was on; her carefully constructed storylines began to unravel, and she teetered on the brink of panic.

Each sound, from the creaking board in the floor to rustling paper cascading down, in her heightened senses, all but taunts at her, reminders of her own spiral downwards. This wasn't just a matter of looking for clues; it was a run-in with her own demons. The serene doctor, a former star in her field, had become a woman haunted by shadows of guilt and fear. Pressing her back to the wall, barely breathing in an effort to slow the wild pace of her heart, Mary understood that she was on a tightrope, setting off in one lie or another, descending into safe concealment or total exposure. In that desperate moment, she realised the truth could be haunting and that sometimes the biggest battles are waged silently in one's own head.

The house felt like an illustration: frozen in time, as if time and the inhabitants themselves were holding their breath until she returned. Her usual presence was gone. There was no pacing or darkening in the rooms, nor was there any whispering of secrets in them. Instead, there was a fat, cushiony silence that fell against the walls, stuffing the empty corners with unspoken secrets. The silence, thick and quiet as if it were breathing, emphasised that something was missing— more than just her body. The air was heavy without that person—heavy in a way that reminds you that there's a world out there taking tugs at your heart.

Attention immediately shifted to where Mila ought to be, it was a void you couldn't ignore. There were the empty chairs, and the untouched glass on the side table, and that faint whiff of her perfume that still clung to a forgotten scarf, all little clues but more than enough evidence that she was not there. It amplified everything that had gone unsaid: the quick pattering of feet that used to resonate here and the furtive glances the survivors stole at one another. Questions just floated in the air like smoke, curling and disappearing before they could even be answered. Dohme's abrupt departure during those crucial hours gnawed at the room's tenuous tranquillity.

The time she had been away was not just missing minutes; it was a loose end that hadn't been retied to the before and after. It always seemed that, if she did not move or speak, the mystery became deeper rather than clearer. This made the people around her suspicious and caused them to doubt her presence simultaneously, as they noticed her absences marked by a characteris-ing mute desperation that grew throughout the day. The entire woman who once was there—the gap be-tween her presence and the vacant departure behind her—turned into a story of its own, fraught with fear and doubt. And in that version of events, the reality of those last hours remained tantalisingly elusive.

The small, almost silent room was humming softly with the sound of fluorescent lights overhead. Careful-ly Byrne's eyes scanned the well-arranged supplies, all securely stored in clear plastic trays. She touched her fingers over the different layers of bandages and medical equipment, firm and sure. The air smelt of disinfectant, a bright, clean-smelling odour that seemed to sharpen her mind as she gazed at each item. It resembled routine business to an observer from outside, yet Byrne under-stood that every little bit counted. Any misalignment or indications of tampering may destroy the case altogether.

Her gloved hand inched farther into the bag, and her eyes narrowed as she peered through its contents. The medical supplies were all in place — until she touched something she had not anticipated. Hidden behind a stack of clean dressings lay a small, smooth glass bottle the size of a man's thumb. Byrne paused a little, catching her breath. The bottle didn't appear special at first glance. It was transparent, and it bore no labels or markings of any kind that would tell you about what it contained. But the way it was set and the fact that it sparkled caught her attention. There was really nothing unimportant in her job. She knew how deadly even the tiniest bottle might be if one had in it the particular liquid that should destroy Julian Vane.

Byrne looked hard at the little bottle as if a secret of one hundred years were in it. The glass was flawless, with no scratches or wear. This type of medicine, an opioid, she knew, could be employed carefully and precisely to help people who were dying feel more comfortable. There was no denying that it wasn't part of the official list. It was like the drug Julian had been given when he got sick so suddenly. Her mind worked quickly over the facts: that Julian had been poisoned, the manner of his discovery, and now this small vial. "It was the one missing thing to really personalise everything. If he was harbouring this drug in secret, it meant that someone had given it to him intentionally, which would indicate that Julian's death wasn't a mere natural decline. Byrne's gut told her Mary's cool, clinical remove was masking something far darker beneath that calm surface.

She lifted the bottle and studied it in the light. The glass was cold and hard, weightless but full of consequence. Byrne's mind raced through the timeline of what had been reconstructed over and over, considering how the medication could have been administered, who might have known and whether Mary had any access to it. She'd learnt that even this one little thing could make all the difference. It was no longer simply about a doctor or a wife; it was about whether someone could slip some hidden poison into what those at the bedside knew would be Julian's final moments. Now she was certain that her suspicions were confirmed: there had been a planned event, and this bottle was the smoking gun that would blow everything open about Julian's death.

The room, quiet and clinical a moment before, now hummed with energy. Byrne gingerly placed the bottle back in the bag, and her mind was already grappling with questions. How did it end up there? How did it get into the med kit without anyone noticing? And what, if anything, did it have to do with Julian's final hours? It would take more digging to uncover the answers, but for now, this little box was about to flip the investigation on its head. She knew that if she wanted to get at the truth, she needed to chase down even the smallest of leads. In situations like this the smallest detail frequently carried the greatest weight, and the whole story was far more complex than it had initially appeared.

This small vial was also a lesson to anyone searching for a solution to the case: occasionally, everything of interest comes down to whatever you're not looking at. Byrne filed the evidence away, well aware that her misgivings were mounting. The silence of the room, the pungent odour of disinfectant and even that glass vial—all told a single story: an act had been premeditated before her, permitting her to discover what was Julian Vane's last, most diabolical gesture.

THE ARREST

Heart racing in her chest, Mary took a quick look around the interrogation room. The dim lighting made the air thick and heavy with the promise of accusation. The press of cold metal against her wrists was simultaneously startlingly foreign and alarmingly familiar, a harsh reminder of how much trouble she was really in. Every fluorescent light above her flickered intermittently, the light patterns and shadows on the dull grey walls making her surroundings feel even more constricting than they already were.

She tried to breathe, to clear her mind and ground herself in reality, but one attempt dissolved the task into thin air and left her lightheaded and disoriented. Hopefully someone here will be able to understand, she thought for one brief, desperate moment, but no face in this room showed any flicker of expression. A voice shouted sharply in the far corner of her mind, asking her questions she could barely hear.

The handcuff echoed in her ears, ringing in her head like a cruel joke. Literally: fear tasted like metal in the back of her throat as she swallowed hard, and she looked down at her restricted hands, praying to whatever god would save her that her heartbeat would slow. How had it come to this?

Why had the world shifted on its axis so violently? Everything in this room was suddenly too still, thousands of seconds congealing into eternity around her. The terrifying moment of clarity, once bright and close, suddenly felt like a phantom hovering in the shadowed corners of her existence. I'll shout, "I swear to you, you are wrong!" but the words jam in her closed throat, but she clamped her hands and handcuffed them against her chest anyway. Cold concrete evidence took root in her lived experiences, twisting and turning the fibres of her life into a criminal tapestry that was no longer alien. She was curled, folded in a foetal position to disappear, but she could not escape the truth of where she was, physically or legally.

The blank glare of the televisions bounced off the shiny conference room tables, casting a ghostly white glow on Sloane's drawn face. Her hands shook a little as she sat, paralysed, while the voice of the news anchor on TV dissolved into a dull murmur. Arrayed on screen was the grainy footage of her arrest, replayed over and over — the cuffs snapping into place around her wrists, the stern faces of officers ushering her through the metal gates of the precinct. It was like watching someone else's life come apart, some woman who bore no relation to the agency she'd built or the careful face she held up. But there she was, caught up in this moment of exposure and humiliation, powerless to do anything other than watch the public witness her fall.

The overhead fluorescent ceiling lights hummed sterile and unforgiving, symbolising the clinical coldness of the new story about to break in countless homes: Sloane, the glossy literary agent, ensnared in a crime scandal. She attempted to slow her breath, but she could feel the weight crushing down into her chest as the truth sank in. But every detail — the way the cameras captured the slight flicker of fear around her eyes, the sharp angles of the shadows on the wall behind her — crushed unceasingly back into her mind. The world was watching and had already decided who she was. Not that woman who'd danced along the edge of financial ruin, who'd deleted emails the way she wiped away fingerprints; just that headline on the screen, a cautionary tale about loss. This was more than exposure; it was a public unravelling she hadn't planned for, at least not like this.

Sloane's head spun with every ignored call, every wild alibi she'd concocted prior to the bust. She thought of the judgment of colleagues, friends and bystanders who had never known her truth, but would now see her face and think "disgrace". It was the sterile smell in the room and the dull murmur of technology that started to get to him. Her mind reeled: what would this mean for Julian Vane's memory? The man whose last story they were each trying so valiantly to control, whose death should have stayed cloaked in calculated mystery? All those delicate stories were now threatened by the barefaced glare of reality — a show she knew in her heart she had no way to shut down.

Beneath the cool facade, a silent storm of panic seethed.

She knew she wasn't just witnessing her arrest; she was witnessing the start of a new fight, one where every word and every image beamed out there could be used against her. The cameras were not lenses of truth but of distortion, and she could do nothing to refocus them. The idea that she might still be able to control the story had struck her as absurd, one more thing getting away from her each time she'd played those cold, uncompromising clips.

Somewhere within a glass-walled room, the "damage control" team (or whatever) began to spring into action like a well-oiled machine that had suddenly realised it couldn't indefinitely put off the day of reckoning. Voices crossed, some sharp and anxious, others calm and insistent. The air was thick, smelling faintly of old coffee as the soft clicking of keyboards bounced off adobe walls. Another headline emerged, adding another layer of social media distortion that transformed Sloane into something unrecognisable with every tick of the clock. The team had a simple mission: rewrite the narrative before it shattered the tenuous legacy that all of them needed.

They moved quickly to create alternative narratives that would tamp down the damage. One team member wrote a statement noting Sloane's long-standing devotion to Julian's career that reframed the arrest as an unfortunate misunderstanding brought on by steadfast commitment. Another wrote carefully worded responses to journalists, subtly casting doubt over the veracity of the charges and insinuating they might have an ulterior motive. From that cause there emanated a policy of damage limitation which was dominated by one single consideration: to save the story about Julian Vane, and consequently Sloane's part in it, from precipitate collapse. To do this, they had to be able to guide public opinion with great delicacy — exchanging animus for empathy and scandal for sadness.

Fictions quietly coalesced in carefully worded press releases, and veiled narrative threads were inserted — hints of artistic pressure, mental health struggles, and personal sacrifice. And the team made sure that this information was handed out not as damage, but as context, drawing Sloane in the picture of a fiercely loyal ally flapping amid a storm she couldn't control. Social media accounts were watched closely, with replies quickly posted under critical comments and hurtful remarks to make sure the conversation did not lead to harmful assumptions. It was an exhausting endeavour, but a necessary one, a frenzied response to the flood of revelation that threatened to drown them all.

While the team spun stories with their web of lies, Sloane sat alone, the pressure of their words weighing down on her. These elaborate lies, which had been fabricated to shield her, only served as a reminder of how thoroughly they'd let go of the truth. The difference between what was real and what wasn't had grown thin, and she wondered how much longer the deception could fly under the radar before it all came tumbling down. But the more she sat watching herself on screen, something quite simply was nailed home to her mind: this fight wasn't about her reputation—it was about her life.

Yet during moments of crisis we all tend to forget how fast a narrative can replicate and gain consciousness. The hardest battle isn't simply that of damage control; it's the war hidden beneath all those feelings, both within and on a global stage. Between remaining grounded, speaking openly with one another, and realising that perception is reality, it can set apart devastation from recovery.

Mila was standing just outside the police station, and her body shook a little from the cold morning air that stung her skin. The strong wind seemed to blow away the last of her stress, leaving her with a strange, short-lived sense of relief. She could finally breathe freely for the first time in what felt like hours, knowing that the worst was over. The thick, grey clouds hung low in the sky, threatening rain. But in her chest, she felt strangely light, as if a weight had been lifted. She held her coat tighter around her as her hands shook, and she looked back at the building with a mix of tiredness and disbelief.

The police had arrested her, told her her rights, and kept

asking her questions. Her heart raced in her chest as they searched her bags, her words caught between truth and panic. But now that she was on the pavement, her mind was racing to figure out what had just happened. The officers said they had arrested someone. But in the middle of all the chaos, she held on to a small bit of certainty. Julian wasn't the person they took away in handcuffs. It couldn't be. She knew him better than anyone else and understood his habits, the little things he did, and how he hid his pain behind a calm, unchanging face. It was a moment of relief, but then doubt set in.

As Mila walked away slowly, her steps felt lighter, like she was walking out of a terrible dream. But that feeling of relief didn't last long. A sickening twist curled up in her stomach, and guilt began to seep into her mind, sharp and unending. The more she thought about it, the more it became clear that they had not only arrested the wrong person, but they had also taken the wrong body from the scene. She looked at her shaking hands and saw how her fingers showed how confused she was. Her mind kept going back to the fight, the push, and the crazy moments right before Julian's head hit the floor. It was a time of chaos, but it was also the time she thought she made him fall. Now that she knew, it was hard to bear. Her storm of guilt was a weight that no amount of relief could lift.

She thought about the evidence—the torn fabric from her sleeve, the way her voice had cracked during that fight, and the trembling in her hand as she ran from the house. Every little thing that had seemed unimportant before now seemed huge. She could clearly remember that night: her voice raised in anger, Julian's quiet defiance, and the shove that made him stumble. Was it enough to make him fall face-first onto the marble floor? The idea made her stomach turn. What else were they missing if they had arrested the wrong man? What aspect of the situation did her own fear and guilt completely obscure? She turned around and looked at the police station behind her. She didn't know if she should go back or hide. She felt the pain of a secret that could destroy her.

The truth was slipping away from her, like sand through her fingers. She knew that Julian's death was planned, but not by her. She knew he had a reason to want out and plan his own death, but she couldn't be sure if her involvement had anything to do with it or if it was just another part of his complicated game. Her thoughts kept going back to that dark manuscript Julian had been working on. Maybe it was his confession. It whispered of a meticulously planned life, of dreams shattered and rebuilt in the shadows. She might have only felt better for a little while, and then the guilt would come back, strong and unavoidable, as she realised that she had unwittingly become a part of someone else's story—an unfinished one that didn't include her at all.

This moment, this cold morning air and brief feeling of freedom, made her weak. She was scared of what would happen to her if she was mistaken about everything, like if the man in the back of the police car wasn't Julian. She knew that the truth was more complicated than anyone else thought. But for now, all she had was this short time of freedom. Soon, though, the weight of her mistake would catch up with her, and she would have to face the awful truth: they had not only arrested the wrong person. They had missed the most important detail of all: the real story that was right below the surface, waiting to be found or buried forever. She realised that guilt was a much heavier burden than relief, and her heart was already feeling its slow, steady grip tighten around her.

Detective Byrne held her ground and narrowed her eyes as she cupped the handcuffs around Mary West's wrists. The loud sound reverberated off the walls of the small, sterile room – giving the moment even more weight. The fluorescent lights above stuttered before coming to life, bathing the two women in stark light. There was the scent of disinfectant in the air, which couldn't be further from the maelstrom of feelings that was going on inside Mary. She seemed almost serene, but there was so much brewing just under the surface. Her eyes gave nothing away.

Everything around them seemed bigger. The officers

bustling in the hall, the dull thud of footsteps on linoleum and an errant printer printing reports were all part of Mary's apparition-inspiring scene. She had quite critically constructed a lie that might save her from the mess into which she had got with Julian. Standing there, the truth was a thousand needles prodding her conscience.

Her fingers trembled slightly, hovering over the small recorder she fingered absently, the one that meant life or death for her. She became aware of the gravity of her situation, and fear gripped her mind. Each second felt longer than the last, as though the universe were mocking her for daring to get a grip on things in such uncertain times. The consequences of her lies threatened to suffocate her, leaving little air for the truth that hid behind the surface.

Although she was outwardly calm, a war raged inside her. She thought about Julian and all the good – his laughter, and intelligence – but also about what she described as bad that had led to a divorce. She was like a tragedienne proceeding towards an inexorable denouement that would shatter the slender gossamer of her existence. Clinging to the father she could no longer see, Mary prepared herself for what was coming with each breath because surely the facts about Julian's death must not only reflect her love for that which is not walking beside her but also a mirror crying out the depths of her fear.

PART III

The Story

CHAPTER TWENTY

THE "STOLEN" STORY

Mary held the hard, cold bench of the holding cell, her thin blouse no match for cold metal. The sterile walls were pressing against her, void of colour or warmth except for the dim hum of an overhead light struggling to keep her from going out. In the stillness, her senses were wired tight to gather in whatever was listening back there, beyond silence: a small shuffle outside in the corridor, the distant tinkle of voices she couldn't quite fit together into words, and the rasp and scrape of someone kicking at linoleum with a shoe. Every sound flitted at the periphery of her senses, a fragile tendril she struggled to hold onto while her brain was processing the disorientating emptiness of her surroundings. Time seemed to stop, extending into a blur of grey immobility as memories tangled and slipped through her mind like ribbons.

Her fingers shook a little, not from fear but from her determination to keep herself in check. In the silence, Mary sifted through broken pieces of the past few hours: whispers of discussions, seconds half-recalled or ducked. In the near-distant city buzz heard from beyond the prison walls, there was something impossibly distant , as if she were living in an entirely different realm – suspended between what had already happened and what she feared might yet be brought to light. The sterile scent hung in her clothes—clean but relentless—a reminder of how far from anything normal this life was, from the hospital halls she had once moved through with a little cocktail of calm certainty coursing through her. Here she was in this small grey world, alone with the echoes of Julian's vanishing presence, a phantom just beyond her grasp inside her head.

Her breathing was slow and even, and she closed her eyes, reaching for whatever remnants of reality might make sense: Julian's absence pressing on her chest, the curl of shame inside it, and the bright stab of helplessness that had characterised her part in all this. The room was cooler now, as though the walls were soaking up her tension and throwing it back at her in physical waves. Outside, life persisted—people spoke, made choices, and assigned blame— but she was caught in a liminal zone where none of that could be true. The faint odour of disinfectant mingled with stale air—a reminder that no matter what story the world was set to reveal itself as next, Mary was at once on the edges of it yet now a passive observer in the baroque complexity of her own life's unravelling chapter.

On the surface, Mary's view was tranquil but delicate underneath, like glass containing a sea. She meditated on her innocence, a word that felt both protective and dangerous within this cell. She could feel the questions circling around her, the assumptions drawn from the evidence — Julian's ill health, the absence of pills, how quickly his life had ended. Sometimes her memories themselves felt horribly incomplete, and it was beginning to feel like something (someone) or even her mind itself had intentionally scattered them by either its will or the very world that was watching and waiting. She told herself that on the stage of reality, appearances counted for everything. What she was after lay beneath layers of fear and regret: shame that she caused Julian's deterioration and humiliation that her dominion had stumbled when her professional façade fell apart.

The pressure of confinement was bearing down on her, physically and emotionally. Being cut off from the people she loved and the chaotic but familiar rhythms of her home felt like yet another punishment. It's those silences that allowed the thoughts to gather about Julian's final moments, what he wanted from all of us and how cruelly unjust it is that the flecks of truth remained just beyond reach, hidden behind a flimsy screen as if intentionally hidden. For Mary, it was not an answer but a threat — an omen of the darkness that hung over her destiny, waiting to be unwound by others who craved control over the narrative. There was a spark of hope that the emptiness would save her from playing any part in the story they were about to force, even if it came at a great cost to her own peace.

Something like defiance stirred deep within her. The ending belonged entirely to Julian, a carefully stage-managed act. Mary's job wasn't the ungodly cause; instead, it was the distasteful stage where she was not the actor but the audience, locked in a vault and required to watch the world present its version of reality while having no say. In that strange in-between, she focused on the small details—the echo of a voice, the creaking of a floorboard, the change in atmosphere—

that someday might break through. Until then, she held her peace, firm and aloof and beyond reach, the keeper of a secret that must be hers alone.

Sloane was in the debris field of her career, gaunt and sweaty. There were crinkled papers and dusty old man-uscripts, and the air sniffed of burnt paper. Shaking her hands, she looked down at the ash that once represented her goals and dreams: charred pieces of what used to be beliefs. It seemed nothing but disaster in silence, a disaster of which every part of her old life was the wreck and ruin. She felt her failures bearing down on her and compressing her like a mantua, pinning both chest and will.

In the still, vacant hours, she couldn't escape the truth any longer. All the things she had slaved for, struggled to build from scratch — now dust and ashes; could nev-er be rebuilt. Her name once meant something in the literary world; it signified sharp insight as well as strong belief. Now, nobody remembered her as anything other than a washed-out agent. Her name withered away in the last vestige of her hope. Everything that had once mattered seemed to mean so little now, and it shocked her. All her brilliance, all the wispy networks of contacts and choked-back tears over issue crossfires that made up her fragile veneer of success were gone now, folded into time and poor judgement.

Their absence was palpable in each corner of her mind. Julian's death, the turmoil in its wake, and her own sense of worthlessness all swirled together into a miasma of regret. She had clung to the idea that somehow her work might define her, but now she knew none of it was real. It wasn't the kind of impact that bursts into flames; just a wearing away of reputation and raison d'etre. Everything else about her legacy was broken shards lying on the floor, like that which remained after a flame had been extinguished. Her tale was of ashes, and that which had given it value — flimsy as paper — had collapsed.

Mila receives the news that her manuscript has been published frozen in place. The words she had allowed to escape from her fingers were let fly into the world, right here on these very pages that flew away from her. Her heart thumped, a tumultuous blend of pride and dread. This, of course, was not just any manuscript; it was Julian's last work, the dark confessions that had tormented her ever since his death. Who better than her to know that he'd written his own story — one of betrayal, manipulation and irreversible consequences? But in her zeal, she was consumed by guilt; she felt as though she were parading a ghost around, merely pulling strings behind the scenes of Julian's tragic denouement.

Her mind was filled with images from the argument, the screaming match that had broken through their brittle veneer of affection and professional camaraderie. Mila could still feel the cold bite of fear from that night, the regret that had seeped into her skin more with each hour. In her eagerness to make a way, she'd stolen that manuscript and thought it would kick-start her career. But she recognised that it was a remnant from a fragile life, one Julian would have preferred to be swept under the rug. Now she faced the truth of seeing his words warp into stories she had never meant to tell.

The whirlwind hit the instant word came of its publication. Text messages arrived from his literary friends, rhapsodising over the terrific novel of sex and drugs that was now the talk of all of New York. Mila was beside herself with excitement. Critics hastened to take Julian's thoughts apart in print, now bearing her fingerprints, along with the stains of a betrayal she might not be able to endure. The reviews were rapturous; Mila felt the heaviness of loss weighing down her chest. Even with the bright articles filling magazine pages and digital platforms, she could practically hear Julian's faraway voice reverberating in her being based on her actions.

The storm had only begun. As the secrets of her manuscript were revealed to the world, so too was her inner turmoil loudened. With every review that complimented the darkness and complexity of Julian's characters, Mila realised she was there, both as a lover and a thief. Her compulsion to tell her side of things only grew more intense, coming into conflict with the fact that telling the truth could dismantle the personal mythology she was working so hard to build. Trapped between loyalty and ambition, the woman she saw was hardly recognisable in her clouded reflection, guilty as sin while spinning in a maelstrom of her own creation.

This influx of enthusiasm in Julian's literary talent was as much a whirlwind to me as what I had felt. Mila's ambition had a voice now, but it was also haunted. Her yearning to make her mark felt like straddling a tightrope bridging a chasm of doubt. The black magic of his manuscript had changed her world. She had sat there with every word read by an audience already hungry for the thoughts from which it seemed the essence of its creator's tragedy had surely been mixed into them. And would any of them even get a whiff of the price that came with it as they oohed over his talent? The boundaries between homage and exploitation grew uncomfortably air-thin, casting huge shadows over the choices she had made with such anguish.

A whirlwind revealed surprises one after the other. Friends became pseudo-friends, their curiosity about the tragedy insatiable. Confidence turned to suspicion when they wondered if this 'new classic' was truly Julian's idea or Mila's stab in the back. Rumours of her involvement danced alongside the praise for the work. Every remark about how brilliant Julian was drove the shards of her heart further inside. Each accolade was also a dirge for a life snuffed out too soon, all for a tale that would forever be tainted with her own darkness – such a fragile transaction; it could unravel at any moment.

In this game of loyalty and ambition, she was winning the world and losing herself. There was no question about the intoxicating feeling of power—publishers came to woo her, anxious to capitalise on the drama surrounding Julian's death and market her as the muse undone. Their steamy chat had been even more sensuous. But amid the glitz, a deep emptiness gnawed at her. The questions about her guilt danced a little too close, an ever-present threat of a game that no longer felt like an art form and had become more of a predatory competition.

Every time she saw the cultural layers of her story unravel, it became increasingly clear to her that silence was not an option. And the manuscript provided her more than a literary platform; it offered an opportunity to finally face the truth behind Julian's last painful goodbye and a chance to unweave his intricate web of lies. But what truth could she — or even would she — reveal? Her quest to create a legacy was now forever entwined with Julian's. The two sides of the stolen success she experienced vibrated through her just as strongly as the type of alienation that reverberated from his void. How long could she continue to ride this tempest in her turmoil-filled mind?

The darkness overlay of ambition and guilt was stifling, but deep in there an ember burnt – a glimmer of hope at redemption found through those pages. It was under her breath that Mila deliberated over where she would go from there and caused the very heart of truth to pass into her story. Those pages would become the vehicle for her grief, a way to face the haunting truth of

Julian's genius and the price of their shared destinies. She understood that while the path would be a heavy slog, she could take pen to paper and write herself a legacy or let others write their lie upon her – an illusion that reality could not tolerate.

With the hum of the interrogation room around her, Detective Byrne leaned back in her chair. It had taken her days of knowing Mary West to understand a wife at the end of her reserves, doing anything she could think of to save a fading husband, fighting what was unbearable in Julian's deterioration. But then, there was the evidence no one saw coming: the faint indications that a seething rage lurks beneath Mary's polished facade. It was not only shame or professional fear that drove her; there was a raw, white-hot anger, buried beneath layers of clinical calm. Byrne's mind scrambled as she slapped together those moments that on the surface appeared insignificant: the clenched jaw when he first questioned them; how Mary's eyes grew heavy with Julian's mention; how frantic searches through medication logs now appeared to be less about innocent concern and more psychological hits of control.

It turned out that Mary's anger wasn't just about Julian's continuing physical disintegration: she was being motivated by something else. It was the grinding powerlessness she kept from everyone, even herself, turned furiously inward. The rage wasn't directed at the disease; it was aimed at Julian's refusal to go gently, at the secrets he harboured and at how his dimming brilliance had come to seem a living reproach of her failure. Byrne gave him time to think about small things: how Mary had ripped up his personal writings, the way she hung around his study sometimes too long, and the smell of dirty clothes and antiseptic that betrayed something deeper than unrest. Mary isn't just looking to protect her reputation; she's seeking ways to reclaim control of a life that's slipping through her fingers.

From there, everything changes for Byrne. Mary wasn't just the stoic wife anymore. She was a woman in the throes of a violent rush of emotion who had let herself do what she needed to do to shut down not only Julian's body but also his voice. The simmering rage Byrne had sensed left a chilling possibility: had this fury driven Mary to cross a line? If so, the tidy narrative of natural causes had come apart at the seams in a hurry, something much darker and far more personal than anyone was willing yet to say.

Mila Novak's world was caving in, however, with as much force as she never dared anticipate. Guilt clawed at her from all sides, damaging every thought in the terrible aftermath of the fight in which Julian's temple was left bruised. From a moment's tension had come blackmail—the secret hold she now had on Julian's still concealed last manuscript. The pages were raw and confessional, full of undeniable truths that, if made public, could destroy more than a reputation. The manuscript was no mere fall from grace; it was a tactical confession of manipulation and cruelty clothed in Julian's genius. Mila possessed a dangerous key, and she turned it over in her hands nervously, knowing that opening the door could make or break her career.

Once the media got a whiff of Mila's participation, the reaction was swift and unforgiving. The headlines blared her involvement in it all, portraying her as the unscrupulous mistress who could have plotted Julian's murder or, at the very least, been part of a deadly secret. Social media bloomed with all manner of theories, snatches of interviews extrapolated into damning narratives, and old footage brought back to sow scandal. Mila's carefully applied veneer breaks under the glare, exposing long-buried guilt that ecstatic readers never knew they wanted her to feel, along with the tough-as-nails go-getter they love to see get their comeuppance. Every new tidbit of gossip added another layer of intrigue, obscuring the true events amidst a sea of conjecture.

The revelation of that secret broke apart fragile alliances and turned all the characters into public figures under the oppressive glare of publicity. Her blackmail, a private struggle for survival and legacy but not exactly freedom, inflamed or incited some larger crisis that had rippled through the lives of those around her. The jarring chaos demonstrated in no uncertain terms that

Julian's death was no longer just a puzzle for the police; it had metastasised into a spectacle, warping reality until nobody could separate truth from falsehood. The media feeding frenzy wasn't just noise — it was a weapon distorting the motivations of characters and driving them toward secrets that could destroy them all.

Chapter Twenty-One

THE FUNERAL

(Two Days Later)

At Julian's funeral, Mary sits under a pale, decaying veil with the feathery folds brushing her cheeks as she tries not to show emotion. Her face, which appears to convey indifference, actually reveals a deeper truth! Instead of a blank canvas, all we can see in it is a decision to be still. All her breath is lilies and wet earth, the scent frothing through the chill air as mourners whisper behind fragile masks and covered faces. The audience are silent, each lost in their own muted thoughts, eyes burning with empathy or judgement or apathy. Their eyes follow Mary, yes, but there is also a palpable measure of judgement in their stares — as if her very presence is some sort of riddle that needs solving. She knows—beneath the apparent solidarity of shared grief—that they perceive her as something else, something darker, more brittle, or possibly even suspect.

And in that moment, Mary's thoughts return to her own secret role in Julian's last gesture — the part she played, whether wilfully or not, in the story he was about to tell. She is very far from the medical office where she works now, having thrown herself into a funeral and a mourning costume. A veil obscures most of her face, but beneath it is an unspoken tension in her jaw and the fine tremble in her hands. She's been advised to be strong, to look untroubled, but her head is swimming with questions. Did they hear her racing heart? Was there a faint ray of doubt in her penetrating gaze? Outside, they see a woman grieving, but inside there is an intricate web of truths, deceptions and terrors suspended. Her being a pariah—wilfully—an outsider forced into the world of mourning—almost seems like destiny, with every footstep she takes away from the crowd feeling like destiny, feeling like exile from her own past life.

Amid the mourners whispering behind elaborate masks, Mary is both detached and too sharply feeling. She goes through the ritual in a numb, leaden state, everything coming into sharp focus in her senses that she would otherwise miss. The coolness of the marble slab pressed against her fingers, the light scent of jasmine and musty paper wafting around her in the air – these feelings are as real to her as anything else she can imagine. Her eyes dart to Julian's closed casket, a harbinger of closure that she can't help but associate with secrets she knows are buried deep within him — and her. It's all anyone can talk about, this terrible thing; everyone is trying to make sense of it in words or silence, but she knows that the truth is much more complicated. Something inside her tells her that she will defend it at all costs – these costs – and this reputation is all she has left.

They describe her as a pariah—a woman ostracised by the very community that once lauded her intelligence and steely composure. Her work, as a cardiologist, is of no solace here. This is the woman with a renowned aura of cool precision, but now she feels naked and vulnerable beneath her public calm. It's like all the eyes in the crowd are spotlights, spotlights, and you'll hear a secret whispered that will be her darkest one. The only thing that anchors her is the understanding that, although she may or may not be innocent about Julian's death, it will be written by her side. She has skilfully crafted her narrative, portraying Julian's death as inevitable and natural, while asserting that it is not connected to her. But behind that stolid mask, she is afraid the truth will unravel from around the edges and show more than she means.

Sloane stood at the door of the funeral home and looked around the room with a deliberate lack of interest. The grey decor fit the sad mood, but she didn't feel sad at all. Instead, her mind went through a list of things she needed to do to keep up the carefully crafted image she had created. She smoothed out her blazer, which was perfectly clean and smooth, as if she were tightening her armour against the emotions that were all around her. Friends and family came together, their faces twisted in sadness, and the air was full of whispers and murmurs. Sloane wrote down the details, like how someone held a tissue and how their voice shook unevenly. This was not the time to share your grief.

She walked through the crowd, giving quick nods as if she were doing a ritual dance, and she always had a cool smile on her face. She didn't love Julian Vane, the dead man, but they had to be together. They had been working together in the unpredictable world of publishing for years, but their relationship had always been businesslike. Sloane changed her mind and decided to keep her emotions locked up while keeping up a professional front. There was no reason for the moment's sadness to get through the veil she wore.

Sloane adjusted the microphone when it was her turn to speak. Her heart was steady. The crowd was quiet, heavy with grief and anticipation. Her voice came out, steady and calm, but it had an unsettling undertone. She started by saying that Julian was a creative genius, and the words came out in a calm way that even she was surprised by. She told a few well-known stories, making sure to choose ones that only showed how outstanding his work was and not who he was as a person.

The words were on the edge of being too respectful, but anyone who was really listening could hear the planned tone. His work made a difference in people's lives. He had a profound, though complicated, understanding of how people feel. He had a difficult time, and that struggle was a big part of his art. Each statement had a purpose: to create a story that hinted at tragedy and made the audience see Julian's death as an artistic sacrifice. Sloane wanted to keep his legacy alive by telling the story in this way. He wanted to make sure that the focus stayed on the work and not the problems that had brought them all here today.

As she went on, her mind raced with what the event could mean. This eulogy was a chance to change how people saw her and tell the story in a way that fit her interests. She discussed the stress that artists have to deal with, which made it sound like Julian's last act was more of an escape than a cry for help. Some people in the crowd nodded in agreement, while others looked at each other with confused looks. After all, who were they to doubt that art could help people deal with things? Sloane stepped down, feeling a mix of happiness and guilt inside her. Even though it meant giving up some truth, her role as the person who put this story together had made Julian's mythology stronger.

Mila was the only one in the gathering around the polished oak casket, and the whispers of the mourners felt like a breeze from far away. She was staring at someplace far away, but her eyes were sharp, as if she were looking at something that no one else could see. Mila's hands shook a little, showing that she was feeling more than just sad. Are you feeling guilty? Need help? It might be both. It flickered behind her serene face, a thin mask that kept her still as she watched the fluttering faces, the shaking shoulders, and the hushed whispers of Julian's death. Everyone was offering their own tale about what happened, but Mila knew that none of them were right.

She could hear parts of speech. One person thought it was an accident, another thought it was suicide, and a third thought it was natural causes. None of these thoughts really went to the essence of what Julian had done. She had promised the dead man in her heart that the truth would stay secret. People would sometimes gaze at her and wonder what she and Julian were to each other.   But Mila didn't move, and her eyes were hard to read.   There was a lot of information behind those eyes that made the world seem both heavy and strangely empty.   She was the only one who had glimpsed behind the curtain; the rest were too busy with their own lives to notice.   In this group of so-called friends and family, she felt both invisible and utterly exposed.

The air was harsh, with the mild coolness of early fall combining with the pleasant smell of fresh flowers and polished wood.   The funeral's calmness didn't match the fury that was going on inside her.   Every whispered theory and sidelong look seemed like an accusation or a question she wasn't ready to answer.   Mila was like a smouldering fire in the back of the room that no one wanted to go too near to.   She reminded me that the truth isn't always clear and maybe it was never meant to be fully known.

Mila drew a big breath later on in the tranquil yard. There were a lot of reporters and cameras nearby, like vultures, and they were all looking for simple solutions to a convoluted subject.   She felt imprisoned between two unseen forces: one that was hidden because she didn't say anything, and one that was clear since she was the only one who knew the truth underneath the pretty surface.   The fragrance of moist dirt stuck to her shoes and mixed with the smell of flowers that had been crushed and were starting to fade. The garden was empty now that time had passed. The shadows became longer as the light faded.   She might think about how much it would cost to stay quiet here, away from the glassy eyes and the microphones that were always look- ing for something.

Julian's death was already turning into something else: a scandal, a news story, or a planned tragedy. The truth he had left behind was too hard and convoluted for anyone to understand.   Mila felt it as a dull pain, like a wound that no one else could see.   The last act wasn't a murder, an accident, or a scream of sadness.   It was a premeditated choice, the last piece of art from a man who wanted to change the story even after he died. She thought about the stolen manuscript that was buried deep in her suitcase. It was a direct confession that may wreck everything. But she hung on to it carefully, knowing how bad it could be for both Julian's legacy and her own.

The air smelt like wet wood and mud, and the withering flowers smelt like sweet and bitter, which made me think of better times. Mila could almost hear Julian's words through the leaves that were moving. That icy, exact tone was what had lured her in and kept her in this risky game. She knew the secret that would ruin the nice stories everyone else told, but admitting it would mean ruining the story people wanted to believe. So she kept in the background, a witness who was both protected and burdened by being quiet. The garden was both a safe place for her and a jail. The sun went down, and the truth settled like leaves dropping. Only those who were bold enough to look closely could see it.

Being near to the truth required straddling a thin line between being seen and not being noticed. Mila knew that sometimes the best narrative is the one that isn't shared, the one that is held close to the eyes that see too much but don't speak enough. At times like these, it wasn't the noise of the crowd or the glare of cameras that made her who she was; it was the steady determination to shoulder the weight of a secret that could never be safely disclosed. To stay alive, she sometimes had to lurk in plain sight, watching and knowing as the world told its own convincing story under her white stare.

Detective Byrne pushed through the huddle, eyes sharp and alert. And then, the awkward silence that settled in on their living room like a thick fog paled only in comparison to the whispered muttering and shuffling of black material at the funeral. There was an undercurrent of feelings that she could sense just below the surface, a stormy sea ready to break its banks. Women were huddled together in groups, with sly, guarded looks on their faces and the flickering of an eye which betrayed a consciousness of guilt or fear or hate. Every small movement — a restless fidget, a quick glance away —

hinted to Byrne that there was more caged behind their veils than they were willing to let people see. She observed how some women clutched at tissues or their purses, as though trying to maintain control through small, physical things. To her, what looked like grief was multiply layered to signify something darker — a fragile veneer that could shatter at any second.

In her opinion, the audience was a perfect viper's nest of women, all smiling with sweet words on their lips. They circled the same safe topics — Julian's life, his work, his sudden death — but beneath it she sensed a toxic undercurrent of suspicion and enmity. The funeral, which was supposed to be a silent tribute, appeared more like a scene in which secrets that longed to be made known were doing battle. Byrne looked on as the wife, Mary, held herself low-key, though her eyes were filled with a latent ferment. The agent, Sloane, remained composed outside even as Byrne briefly detected a glint of desperation behind her composed facade. Mila, the love interest, looked more breakable and skittish, less in control of herself. Each woman was secretly assessing the others, weighing the values and secrets of their silent allies and enemies.

She reflected on how the funeral had become such a delicate battlefield, where allegiances could be transformed in an instant. There was real sorrow in the women's faces, but their grief was mixed with something else—maybe shame, guilt at not being able to face the plain truth. In that fragile space, lies could be disguised as sincere mourning. Byrne knew that beneath the veneer of friendship, petty jealousies and long-held resentments simmered just below the surface, skirting a fire held just under a light sheen of snow. Julian's death had turned into more than an end; it was a mystery that illuminated the ugly, complicated truths inside each woman, truths that could come bursting out at any moment if someone pushed them just right. The funeral became a high-wire act, every woman knowing that one more word or movement might undo what they had worked so tirelessly to suppress.

The scene was a tense world, and Byrne knew it, the feeling of it sometimes more like home to him than anywhere else: the watching and listening; piecing together all the pieces of stories that had as many holes as bits told. Her practiced eyes caught subtle details: Mila's balled fists, holding her clutch with teeth-bared tenacity; Sloane's stiff smile that didn't reach her eyes; Mary, standing at attention but clamping down on a clearly built panic. All these little clues indicated that none of these women were merely innocent mourners. ' Their demeanour, characterised by an inability to meet others' gazes or an excessive display of tears, revealed that they were concealing recent secrets. Byrne had seen this tendency before — how grief muddies the delineations of guilt and innocence, turning friends into enemies in an instant. The truth was buried beneath all their masks, and she was here to strip those layers away one by one, no matter how hard or hazardous it might be.

In each of these cases, Byrne noted that a surface was telling only one sliver of the story. Under the veneer of such well-composed smiles, each woman harboured her own concealed motives— her own set of untruths to bring out when the time was right. Her instincts convinced her that the funeral was not, in fact, the end of anything but a staged prelude to something much darker. Some of the women could be squabbling about inheritance, others about shame or guilt they denied. A couple, Byrne suspected, may have an even more treacherous secret beneath the grief—a lie so fundamental it would alter everything if exposed. The combination of emotions, stifled motives and unspoken dangers made the event a ripe breeding ground for secrets. Byrne knew that the real case was taking place under her feet, in the silences between words, where he was stripped bare and Fortuna had formed a viper's nest.

CHAPTER TWENTY-TWO

THE RECORDER

Mary sat in the half-dark study and experienced waves of nostalgia and sadness. Bookshelves sagged under the weight of Julian's literary accomplishments. Specks of dust flittered in the shafts of sunlight, sneaking through the partially open curtains. She inhaled, letting the warm scent of old paper and cold coffee wash over her frame. With every creased sheet of paper and dog-eared book that went into a cardboard box, she could feel another sliver of her past snapping off.

She couldn't get rid of the sense of isolation that settled in her chest. There was Julian's cheek as she worked her way slowly through the mess. Every object — a coffee mug stained with old brew, a typewriter whose keys were no longer readable, loose pages of manuscripts scrawled on in red ink — was a story, one small piece of the life they once had together. Memories came to her, both sweet and bitter, twining through the sharp edge of loss. She stopped, her fingers touching a picture frame that used to hold their wedding photograph. Almost, she heard Julian's laughter in the room somehow, a cruel reminder of what she had lost.

As she packed the papers neatly into boxes, Mary's hand encountered something odd – a small, chill object lodged between two reams of paper. It caught her interest, and she pulled out a voice recorder, marred by a series of long, deep scratches that seemed to have weathered it through the ages. What could Julian have recorded? Her heart thumped as she cupped it in her hand, a bit of him ever familiar yet alien. She took a nervous breath and hit play, the device coming to life.

There's this odd void that happens when Sloane Porter walks into a room — lack of presence and voice. Unlike the living tension animated between Mary, Mila and even Detective Byrne, Sloane does not contain a player caught in the spike of sudden pressure from Julian Vane's death. She's not struggling with the gut-wrenching grief, the beating self-blame or the frenzied quest for answers. She doesn't; she lingers at the edges, a dark reflection of this moment whose importance is discreetly obliterated. The urgency, the shattered memories and twisted emotions in the span of time following Julian's final act seem to fly past her, unfilling those stories within that frame. The absence is not a lack but a void — an omission, that is, in the story that elsewhere darts with competing voices.

Sloane's is a story of control and calculation in the world that occurs offstage, not within the chaos of the immediate aftermath. Her fall to poverty and wild attempts to recover Julian's reputation take place elsewhere, down dark corridors where Mary halts in indecision or Mila grasps at crumbling manuscripts. If Mary represents the frantic need to shield one's reputation, and Mila represents panic and betrayal, Sloane embodies coolly methodological survival—a cold equation not yet present in those raw hours of emotional chaos after Julian's death. No recorder clicks on in the calm for her; no confession or regret leaks from her lips at the breaking point. Her absence in this chapter is a detail only in its absence— an unread letter among the pile of them, a phantom motive free to whisper somewhere else.

Her thing in this second is a gentle reminder that every story has absent pages and every side holds darkness. As she is tacked into the larger mystery of what happened at Julian's end, here she is again stranded outside the room where truth is being brought to light, a mute protagonist biding her time to disclose that which once was concealed. Readers will miss her presence nearly as viscerally as the tension that can be seen between the other three women; it's a silent reminder that no story is ever fully contained in one space or moment, and some stories stubbornly refuse to fit with the urgency pressing in on them from outside in the hours after death. In so doing, Sloane's "not applicable" presence deepens the novel's examination of memory's limitations and our shape-shifting relationship to time.

One pragmatic realisation to take away is that silences and omissions, as much as spoken words, help structure our understanding. Hearing the counter can only open up some hidden agendas and secrets, they don't want to reach out. Just as it can sometimes be as illuminating to watch for what isn't said, listening to what's not taking place provides a picture all its own.

Trembling slightly, Mila pulled out the cluttered desk drawer, and his hand brushed over crumpled receipts and cold coffee-stained papers before she found what she was searching for – a petite, humble little voice recorder. The device weighed more than it seemed as though it should, its plastic surface worn from years of use, but there was a quiet promise to it. The smell of old paper and dried coffee wafted up around her, and she closed her eyes to keep from getting even more anxious. She unpinned the tape and touched the button, attempting to take deep, steadying breaths as she uncapped the device, her fingers shaking along its cool plastic. Every ambient noise seemed to fall silent around her, and she stopped breathing when a muted thump from the source inside that little device reached her ears.

As her heart raced, she hit the play button, instantly filling the silent room with the faint crackle of Julian's voice. It was unsteady at first, as if he was struggling to rein in his emotions, but then it firmed up and became cooler. Mila's ears perked, hearing every word, pausing, trying to monitor each inflection as Julian began to sound...different—a different that made her belly cold. She knew that he was playing, teasing, and lording over even in his silence. As he spoke, so cautiously intentioned, she was hearing something from him she never had before, faced quite like this. His voice, low and measured, resonated off the wooden planks, filling the dim room's negative space with shadow. In that instant, Mila understood that this was not merely a recording but an endgame, a piece of careful choreography that had enmeshed her in a web of deceit she could still barely comprehend.

As the shaky voice filled the room — the words almost whispered — she played the recording again, as if hoping to find some significance in nuances of cadence. Julian was a master of the puzzle, his words pieces that all eventually filled gaps. Every silence, every pause (was) loaded with intent. When his "final decision" exited his mouth, it dangled in the air like some weird lilt, full of regret and resolve. Slightly bitter sarcasm crept into his tone, mixing with an eerie detachment that revealed the workings of his mind. The manner in which he teased the silence made it seem as though he wanted whoever was there to appreciate the gravity of his decision, staging an exit worthy of a master. The desk lamp's weak light flickered and stretched long shadows while Mila leaned nearer, her heart hammering against her ribcage. It was only then, for the first time, that it occurred to her that he had left her a trail—a secret message designed as one last troubling truth in need of decoding.

Detective Byrne sat forward at her desk, eyes narrowed with focus. Hundreds of case files on his desk – any one of them could clear the air around his death. Her desk lamp's weak light threw some sharp shadows that only accented the clutter in the small office. A mug of half-drunk coffee rested perilously close to the edge, a testament to hours spent staring down evidence, pursuing rumours. Beside it sat a newly found voice recorder, tiny and streamlined amid the wreckage. This was no mere doodad; this was a potential game changer in a case that had already dominated her thoughts for days.

As she unfolded the first file, an overwhelming sense of recognition came over her. Photos of chalk outlines were splayed out before her: cold, clinical. The sight of Vane in a pool of red beneath the bright lights had been gruesome. The reports outlined the early theories: natural causes, an accidental overdose or some kind of terrible suicide. Both scenarios tugged at her thoughts, but something wasn't sitting right. She felt the little shifting moments escaping her grasp like the shadows that slid around the edges of her office. The voices of the three women—Mary, Sloane, and Mila—seemed almost to be speaking directly to her, three individual stories spun out before her from a single source and all hiding more than they revealed. Then her eyes were drawn to the flash of the voice recorder, and she was having no part of it.

Byrne took a deep breath and hit play on the recorder, its crackling sound cutting through the stillness of the room, pregnant with dread. If anything, the poor audio only served to highlight the desperate tone of Vane's voice. He said it with clarity that sent a cold shiver down her spine, threading his words through her own. Her heart pounded as she read every word, the enormity of their implications descending upon her like a leaden shroud. It was no mere confession; it came across as a finely wrought performance for an audience that prided itself on loving the theatre. The more she heard, the more she understood how carefully calculated had been every pause and faltering syllable to influence not only his destiny but also those of three women mourning him.

The more she plunged herself into the recording, the clearer it seemed: Julian had not simply died; he had made a story, one that cast his life and death as part of a final, sorrowful work. His desire for legacy and control oozed from every word. It was unnerving to think how deliberately he had calculated this. He was both part of the down-and-outers he sang about and pulling strings from beyond the grave, making sure his life would be a riddle that beguiled and perplexed those he left behind. Detective Byrne felt as though she were not listening to a victim but the architect of deceit. Her fists balled at the realisation that dawned on her. The perfect murder wasn't about blood; it was about storytelling, and Julian had penned the last chapter himself.

CHAPTER TWENTY-THREE

THE VOICE-MEMO

THE FIGHT

Mary held the phone close to her ear. The soft crackle of the voice memo filled the quiet room like a storm breaking overhead. Mila's clipped and tense voice, cutting through the heavy words exchanged with Julian, stopped her breathing. The argument had sharp edges, and the voices rose and fell like waves crashing in slow motion. Their tone was brittle; anger was held tightly beneath a fragile calm that broke with small cracks of accusation. The dull thud of something hitting wood and the brief scuffling that Mary heard outside of the voices made her skin crawl.

Every sound had meaning. The speaker picked up on the muffled footsteps, sharp exhales, and the sudden, unmistakable grunt of someone in trouble. It was raw and unfiltered, rough and terrible, like a private fight that had been ripped open and put right in her ears. Mary's fingers shook a little, as if the stress could jump out of the phone and grab her. She could feel the tightness in her chest, like someone was drowning silently but gasping for air. Then there was the quick retreat—Mila's quick steps faded into the distance, like an echo fading into the dark. Mary felt colder all of a sudden. The sound of a door closing far away reminded her that she was alone with this recorded storm.

The silence around Mary got louder as the voices faded. Mila's footsteps as she ran away weren't just the end of a fight; they were the beginning of something darker, a crack that she didn't think could ever be fixed. Mary stayed still, and even after the tape stopped, she could still hear it in her head. Her heart raced in a way that was somewhere between fear and disbelief.

Before the shove, the tension was almost too much to handle. Mary thought about how heavy the moment felt, like the kind of pressure that makes your skin crawl and your lungs tighten. Then, out of nowhere, the recording picked up the unmistakable sound of a shove: quick, strong, and completely real. She could hear the crash clearly in her ears; it was a loud thump against the floor that shook her like a sudden blow. It was the kind of noise that made her gasp without thinking about it and sped up her heart rate, as if she were there, watching the scene unfold in fast motion.

After that, there was a short, tense silence, as if the world was waiting for something to happen. Then Julian's voice came back, this time steadier. He was out of breath but somehow calm in the middle of all the noise. She could hear him get up, hear his body move, and hear the floorboards creak a little bit under his weight. Julian was still there, strong, calm, and in control, even though there had been a fight, a fall, and a shock. The way he moved showed that he had thought about every second and that he was not going to let what had just happened get to him.

Finally, the sound of the door locking softly but deliberately broke up the soundscape. It was a small act, but it was full of meaning, like putting up a wall to keep the outside world and everything unwanted out of the room. That lock wasn't just for security; it was a statement, a final barrier against anyone who wasn't invited. Mary could tell how carefully Julian had planned his last few acts by how he controlled what people saw and heard. The recording was over, but the shove, the fall, and the lock were still clear and heavy in her mind.

Mary (listening): Julian's voice. "It's not enough." He confessed that he has a neurological disease and revealed his last plan. He hears him hit his head, plant drugs, and say, "Let them tell the story..."

Julian's voice suddenly broke through the thick silence in the room. It was sharper and more commanding than anyone had expected. It was almost like a ghost was hiding just below the surface of his voice, which would slip into the fabric of a conversation. It wasn't loud, but it was heavy. It went through the spaces between words and settled deep in the listener's mind. Some nights, when everyone thought he was lost in thought or far away, he would talk to himself in a soft voice, as if he were telling secrets to himself. Other times, his voice was frantic, and he spoke in sharp sentences that showed he was on edge. Now, in those last moments, his voice had a strange power, like a last message from someone who knew they were about to leave everything they knew behind.

Julian's confession came out slowly, in a jumbled mess of words that hinted at something darker hiding behind his public face. He had said, in a quiet, almost worn voice that echoed in the room's silence, "It's not enough." Those words felt heavy, like he was admitting to a failure that went beyond his writing or reputation. Later, when the investigators put together his mental state, they found signs of a neurological disease—most likely a slow, steady decline that he had kept hidden from most people. His words seemed like a desperate attempt to gain attention before his body completely failed him. He knew he was losing himself, his mind slipping away day by day, and he didn't want to be remembered as someone who was sick and lost.

Julian would often hit his head softly when he was feverish and shaky. It was a nervous tic that got worse as the days went on. The sound of his hand hitting his skull mirrored the pain he was unable to express verbally. He may have done it to punish himself or to calm himself down in the middle of the chaos of his mind. He would sometimes mumble strange words that sounded like pieces of a story that only he understood. And then there were times when he would hide small amounts of drugs in places he knew no one else would look. These actions weren't random; they seemed to be components of a carefully devised plan. It was as if he was trying to control his ending in a way that no one else could.

One night, as the shadows grew longer in the room, Julian sat by himself with a low, shaky voice. His eyes looked far away and unfocused, but they also seemed to be full of a cold clarity. He suddenly whispered to himself, "Let them tell the story..." His voice echoed through the room, full of meaning. It wasn't just a request for control over the story; it was a statement of defiance. Julian didn't want anyone else to decide how he died; he wanted it to be a story he told. You could hear a faint scraping sound as he spoke. He was hitting his head again, in a slow, deliberate rhythm that could have been a warning or a sign. His hands shook as he leaned forward and pressed the back of his head. His voice was barely audible, but it was full of determination. The words hung in the air after he stopped, echoing in the silence and giving off a cold sense of his final intent.

Later, in the quiet of the night, someone found him parked on the edge of his bed, still alive but unconscious. The scene was almost like a doctor's office, with pill bottles nearby and a faint smell of bitter medicine in the air. Earlier that day, Julian had put drugs in his medical bag. At first, this seemed like an innocent thing to do, but then his strange words made sense. Every scar and tremor on his body revealed a story he hoped would remain untold. What was most troubling, maybe, was his wish to write his ending, to make the perfect final scene that would last even after he was gone. And that's what made the mystery so scary: Julian had become the master of controlling his story, even after he died, leaving a trail of clues that only those who looked closely could figure out.

His last act was small but planned. Some people thought he had fallen into a deadly sleep, while others thought it was just a sad accident. But Julian had planned his departure with the same care as a writer planning the last chapter of a book. He made up a story about a neurodegenerative disease that was taking away his memories and motor skills. The real reason he wanted to leave was to leave behind a story so complicated and layered that no one could say they understood it completely. His last words, his last touches, and his hidden notes all showed that he was a man who wanted to control his legacy even though his body was falling apart. When the investigation reached a turning point, the truth came out in a whisper: Julian had planned his death as a final, sick work of art. It hit me hard: Julian wouldn't give up control, even after he died. He wrote his story on his terms.

THE VOICE-MEMO

THE "TRUTH"

There was dead silence in the room when Julian's voice rang out, loud and sharp and commanding in a way no one had expected. His voice had a tendency to blend into the weave of conversation, kind of like a ghost hanging just behind stitched seams. It was not loud, but it landed somewhere— between the words and in the listener's mind. At times on those nights, when he was certain no one else could hear him or had already fallen asleep, he would talk softly to himself, as if sharing secrets. Occasionally, his voice became frantic, punching out short sentences that revealed a mind on edge. Now, in those waning moments, his voice had a strange gravity to it, like a final proclamation from one who knew he would leave everything he knew behind.

Slowly, however, Julian's confession unravelled; an impenetrable web of garbled words that suggested to Jackson just how deeply troubled the soul behind his public face really was. It's not enough," he had told me, a quiet, almost weary statement that reverberated in the room's stillness. He spoke those words as if they were heavy, as though he was conceding a loss that extended beyond his writing and reputation. Much later, when researchers reconstructed what was happening inside his head, the clues led to a neurological disease — likely a long, slow decline he had hidden from nearly everyone. They were the last desperate request of a blind man, to be listened to before his body failed him completely. The fact of the matter was, he knew he was losing himself, that his mind was going day by day, and he didn't want to be remembered as someone felled by illness.

Feverish and off-kilter, Julian frequently banged his head lightly — a nervous tic that intensified with each day that passed. The hollow noise of his hand striking the side of his skull rang out painful things he could not say. It was self-punishment or maybe a way to keep himself rooted in the chaos of his unravelling mind. Other times he mumbled things to himself, odd phrases that sounded like pieces of a story no one else knew. And then there were times that he would deposit small amounts of drugs in various places, thinking carefully about places where he knew no one else could find them. Those were not random acts of self-destruction—they felt like parts of a final, measured plan, as if he was trying to control his ending in the sort of way that no one else could.

One evening, when the shades lengthened in an angle of the room, Julian sat alone with a low and trembling voice. There was something remote and far-away in his gaze – a lack of focus, yet an icy kind of sharpness at the same time. Then, suddenly, to himself: Let them tell the story... His voice dropped in upon the room like something more than sound. It wasn't just a plea for narrative control; it was an act of defiance. He wanted his death to be a tale he wrote, not an accident or tragedy another might script on his behalf. As he spoke, you could hear the soft scrape of something hard against the wood — he was thumping his head once more, in a slow, deliberate rhythm that may have been a warning or some kind of symbol. His hands shook as he leaned forward on the back of his skull, voice hardly more than a whisper but firm. The words hung there, a ghostly echo in the hush that followed as he went silent, and they were cold with what might have been his own last wish.

And later when the night was quiet, someone found

him parked on the edge of his bed, unconscious but alive. The scene was almost clinical — pill bottles close by, a whiff of bitter medicine in the air. Earlier in the day, Julian had stashed drugs in his medical supplies, which seemed like a harmless exchange at the time but suddenly clicked with his words. His body was a map of secrets, a series of scars and tics that told their tale in bits and pieces that he hoped would never be fully connected. Most of all, perhaps, he felt the urge to shape his own ending — a final scene so perfect that it could outlast even his own mind. And indeed, that's what made the mystery so creepy—Julian had mastered narrative control even after he died, leaving a trail of clues only really discernible to those who took the time to look.

His last move was mild but intentional. To some it seemed he fell into an immortal sleep; to others, a fatal one. But beneath it all, Julian had scripted his exit with the precision of a literary author plotting the final chapter in a novel. The neurodegenerative disease that had been raiding his memories and moving parts wasn't actually robbing him of anything, he said: it was just a cover story — the real goal was to leave behind a narrative so multilayered and confounding, no one could say they totally got it. His last words, final touch, hidden notes — all spoke of a man who desperately wanted to manage his legacy even as his body betrayed him. And then, when the inquiry finally turned a corner, the awful truth was whispered—Julian had faked his own death—in one final distorted work of art. It was a shattering realisation: even in death, Julian would not surrender his dominance, rewriting his narrative on his own terms.

THE NEW "REALITY"

The room she is in seems suffocating, like layers of past and future are crowding her from all directions. She can almost feel the murmurs of history powering those moments of pain and betrayal that brought her here, to this crucial moment where truth meets narrative. The ticking of the clock is deafening; it's a constant reminder that time is running out and one minute can make all the difference.

Julian loved the stories his life could tell, the way he twisted them into something epic and significant. But what had he actually left behind? His genius was diminished by his last act — a self-made tragedy designed to ensnare those he loved most. Mary muses on what she has; memories alone can be distorted and bent into a filler narrative the majority would like. But what is a story worth if it must be purchased at the expense of reality? She squirms, the morality of her impending manoeuvre clearly troubling her.

Was she betraying Julian or simply saving herself from a destiny inextricably linked to a truth so convoluted that none could fathom? In this instant, a wave of relief and horror sweeps over her as she realises how much that decision could change. Julian had scripted an ending to his life like a play, and she was the lead actress all of a sudden in words she hadn't composed.

With the recorder off and finality sinking in, Mary feels the atmosphere around her: thick, electric. The world out there still isn't paying attention; they're lulled by easy mythologies into feeling secure. But there she is, standing in a web of deception that spans from her husband to who she herself even is. She can already see the headlines: "An Artist's Tragic Death" or "The Demise of a Genius". Each one a story, each one a twist away from the truth she knows. In that moment, Mary grits her teeth and braces for the future she's wrought – one woven of shadows and whispers where truth may never find its way home.

The desk lamp's dim light made long shadows in the messy office, which smelt like old coffee and was full of papers. Sloane's grip on the phone got tighter, and the call was crackling a little because she was so far away from the person on the other end. Her voice broke the silence, steady but sharp enough to carry the weight of her choice: Forget Julian. Mila Novak is the real story. I'm signing her. There was no hesitation or doubt in that one statement. She leaned back for a moment, her eyes narrowing as the finality of the words filled the room. A new pulse of determination broke the silence.

People had been discussing Julian's death for days. People were whispering theories and making guesses in quiet voices, all mixed up with the mess of his fading legacy. But Sloane had seen through the surface, the manufactured grief and performative tragedy. The pieces of the puzzle weren't fitting together anymore; a new shape was forming under the noise. That shape was Mila Novak, a young, fierce woman who was breathing in Julian's shadow while telling her own, sharper story. The present was the story that mattered most. Her gut told her that Mila was the key to getting back everything that had been lost because of Julian's death. And she wasn't going to let anyone else say it first.

For a moment, the queue was quiet, but then Sloane spoke again, bringing the person back into focus. No matter what, I'll get Mila on board. She has real power; the rest is just noise. Her voice got softer, and a rare hint of urgency came through, showing the adrenaline that was building up inside her. The mission was more than business; it was a last chance to make things right and get back on her feet in a world that was quick to write her off. Julian was getting weaker, but Mila was getting stronger, and Sloane was ready to catch her before she reached the dizzying heights Julian had fallen from.

Sloane's voice stayed calm, but her mind raced with all the things she needed to do. It wasn't just about finding talented people to sign Mila Novak; it was also about controlling the story that would take over the literary world next. She knew Mila's story better than anyone else. She knew about her complicated relationship with Julian and the guilt that was almost palpable in every word she said during their short, tense meeting. Mila's every move was full of ambition, and there were sharp, dangerous secrets waiting to be revealed. That unstable mix made Mila perfect for a story that would sell itself, but it also meant that Sloane had to act quickly and wisely.

She thought about writing the pitch, a dark, deep story full of hidden regrets and whispered betrayals. Mila's rise from the ashes of Julian's fall wasn't just going to happen; it had to happen. The story would draw readers in not with flashy plot twists or violent confrontations, but with the slow build-up of personal pain and changing loyalties. Sloane knew that this story would make readers think about their beliefs and make them wonder what was true and what was a carefully crafted lie. It was the kind of story the world needed, one that kept you coming back for more and more each time.

Sloane laid out the first steps as she spoke: secret meetings with Mila, setting up interviews that blurred the lines between confession and performance, and keeping the competing stories going just enough to keep people's interest but never letting it boil over. She would take back control of Julian's legacy by focusing the public's attention on Mila's guilt and ambition. It wasn't just a business plan; it was a way to get back control. If Mila's truth became the accepted story, Sloane would rise with her, making herself the force behind the year's most mysterious and gripping literary sensation.

The timing, the whispers, and even the spaces between the lines were all important. Sloane knew that with Mila's story, she wasn't just selling a book; she was selling an experience and a voice that made readers question what they thought they knew about truth and memory. Mila possessed a unique advantage in this complicated story that no one else could match. And Sloane was ready to make sure no one else got to it first. The phone call ended, but the plan was already in motion. The change in focus was as clear as the faint smell of rain on the windowpane in the dark office.

Sometimes, the best stories aren't the ones that make a lot of noise. They're the ones that make you feel uneasy and stay with you long after you've finished reading them. When you realise that everything you thought you knew might be wrong, that's when a story really grabs you. As Sloane made the call, she knew exactly what kind of story she wanted to tell: one based on bits of truth, hidden secrets, and the complicated, some-times dangerous relationship between guilt and ambition. It was the kind of story that changes lives, shifts power, and leaves everyone a little different in the end.

Mila was in the middle of her tiny hotel room, sorting and stacking her clothes. The smell of fresh ink and a faint hint of cigar smoke wafted through the room, saturating the air in a combination of creativity and late-night thinking. On the bed, her suitcases were half packed — a neat allusion to her thorough nature. Each item was chosen with intention: two silk blouses, a pair of dark jeans and her favourite scarf. She glanced one last time at her phone for reminders, and ahead of her lay a blur of events — interviews, book signings, conversations that would fill the next few weeks. She straightened her blazer, working through the stories she would tell, hunting for the phrasing with which to interest her audience, perhaps even suggesting that they might suspect some of the truths behind this story and the tale she wished to tell.

"Alright," she sighed, a content grin forming on her face as she moved over to the small desk by the window, littered with promotional flyers and other paraphernalia. Handbills, bookmarkers and press clippings, stacked neatly in a row. She practiced her opening lines in a hushed tone, getting her voice ready—trying not only to sound confident but also herself. Her fingers shook as she lifted a card with her speaking notes, excitement and nerves fluttering in the pit of her stomach. There was something different about the upcoming tour – more personal, more layered than before. She knew each interview could mean potentially revealing something about herself she hadn't meant to, or even worse: giving up secrets she couldn't afford to have divulged. The crowd was excited, and a part of her wondered if she could hold up under the pressure of their interest and her doubts.

Mila's mind flickered back to the fight she'd had with Julian only a few days earlier as she read over her documents. She tasted the bitterness of coffee in her mouth and remembered how quickly she had fled his house, holding his manuscript close to her chest. She knew the truth: the fight had been an ugly one; she could have overreached with her words during their argument. At times she questioned if her fears and guilt were clouding her judgement. Did she truly cause his fall? Or was it merely another incident in a long line of inexplicable moments? Her eyes—wide and dark, the need inside them unspoken, a torrent bottled behind her lips as every request she dared not make of him surged past its restraints too long in place—stared back at her until Elena found herself contemplating whether or not she could face the role she had played in Julian's tale. The dark manuscript, her insurance policy and her curse lay somewhere in the bag, waiting to be deployed or abandoned. Her burden of secrets was heavy as she took her final steps into the future before they opened these doors, when nothing at all would ever be the same.

It was late in the afternoon, and Detective Byrne sat behind her desk cluttered with case files as the sun peered through the blinds, creating stripes against them. They heard not the familiar astir of their precinct, but dead quiet above and around! She rolled back in her chair and sifted through the hard copies. Every item felt like it was calling out for her attention. Images of Julian Vane's lifeless body, the prescription bottles and witness statements swirled about her head in a vortex of confused chaos but one thing was very plain to Belle; All that evidence had been stacked up against Mary West. As a cardiologist, Mary's cool and undeniable confidence felt almost too perfect compared to the storm of suspicion looming overhead. Yet Byrne had a nagging sense that there was more to unearth beneath the surface. The facts bore that out, heavily and inescapably, making a narrative suggestion not only of Mary herself as the arch enemy but also as the magnate of all Julian's destruction.

Byrne had dedicated untold hours to poring over records, and the scales of justice were tilted heavily in one direction. Witnesses had seen Mary by the apartment earlier on the evening Julian died. "Witnesses indicate," said the Post, that the fact that she remained and was in a suspicious posture when arrested kept Byrne's resolve stoked. And the medication discovered at the scene — a combination of opioid painkillers and anti-anxiety drugs — brought focused attention to the entire problem. Mary's expert skills made her a leading suspect; could a woman whose only intense learning was in the intricacies of medicine have been so coldly calculating? Detective Byrne thought about the implications: the deep strata of professionalism it would take for a woman to lean on her husband's life this hard. It was cold and creepy but so mesmerising it made her want to pick at the seams of Mary's perfect life.

Tension crackled in the DA's office as Detective Byrne presented her case. The walls around her, covered in plaques and case resolutions, testified to the gravitas of her beliefs. Her tone was confident as she laid out the evidence against Mary West.

"We've got an ironclad case," she said emphatically, looking the DA in the eye, with the DA leaning forward nervously tapping a pen on his desk. The tension in the room was thick as Byrne flicked through the papers on her desk, ready to clear up some of the ambiguity that clouded over everything.

"Look at the timeline—" she began, gesturing toward a chart covered with annotated notes and arrows. "Mary was the last one to be seen with Julian. The person who put her at the apartment has no reason to lie. The medicine — her medicine — was in his system along with something that she couldn't script without getting raised eyebrows. It's too good to be true; this is lining up way too perfectly."

Every point she hit felt like a stepping stone toward a conclusion, pushing the narrative closer to finding someone guilty. The way Mary had attempted to manage the narrative was very telling of her character. Though her clinical mind might argue for innocence and the possibility of extending a life, Byrne does not seem done with that control, and beneath the effort there was something cop-like about the setup Byrne wanted to take down.

Byrne could almost see the DA thinking through the options. Would they take the facts to be as they were?

Or would they need to hear more before pressing for an indictment? The stakes were high, and Julian's sad story seemed fated to echo in perpetuity without resolution. The motive, she thought, was as strong as the evidence; being constantly under a magnifying glass could but drive to madness anyone who floated near the bed-lamite's brink.

"Mary's career would absolutely crumble under the weight of scrutiny. Alone, that might be enough for her to take desperate measures," Byrne prodded, trying to kindle the fire of urgency in her colleagues.

Could they convince the D.A.? It could be brought to believe that one's truth might rivet like an artist's final performance, if only they could hustle this case up and ahead before the grief about Julian Vane filled in with swarthy untruth.